BUCKSKIN RUN

BUCKSKIN RUN
LOUIS L'AMOUR

BANTAM BOOKS
TORONTO · NEW YORK · LONDON · SYDNEY

BUCKSKIN RUN

Bantam racksize edition / December 1981

Louis L'Amour Hardcover Collection / November 1981

ACKNOWLEDGMENTS

The stories contained in this volume were previously
published in slightly different form.

"The Ghosts of Buckskin Run," in Thrilling Ranch Stories,
May, 1948.

"No Trouble for the Cactus Kid," in Texas Rangers,
December, 1947.

"Horse Heaven," in Range Riders Western, 1950.

"Squatters on the Lonetree," in Texas Rangers, July, 1952.

"Jackson of Horntown," in Texas Rangers, March, 1947.

"There's Always a Trail," in Exciting Western, July, 1948.

"Down the Pogonip Trail," in Exciting Western, May, 1949.

"What Gold Does to a Man," in Thrilling Western,
January, 1951.

Book designed by Renée Gelman.

This book may not be reproduced in whole or in part, by
mimeograph or any other means, without permission.
For information address: Bantam Books, Inc.

ISBN   0-553-06226-3

Published simultaneously in the United States and Canada

PRINTED IN THE UNITED STATES OF AMERICA

0   9   8   7   6   5   4   3   2   1

To Jack Evans

CONTENTS

INTRODUCTION

The stories in this collection are fiction based upon a knowledge of events of a similar nature. The Historical Notes are exactly that, bits of western violence lifted from the day-by-day lives of western people. It was not, as many have surmised, a lawless time. The duel was, in many quarters of the world, still the accepted method of settling disputes. However, at the time of the gun battles related here the days of the Code Duello were at an end.

Often I have been asked if such gunfights actually took place, for there are those who believe such stories are the stuff of fiction, or invented by makers of motion pictures. Several writers have attempted to list the gunfighters and the gunfights, and one author has listed 587 gun battles, and has done it well, but there were at least four times that many in the period from 1850 to 1910. None of the gun battles in my historical notes, for example, are included in that book. To list them all is difficult, if not impossible, yet we do have the files of old newspapers, court records, coroners' reports, and diaries, which are helpful.

It is well to mention, however, that ninety percent of the gun battles took place in either saloons, the red light district, or out on the range, having little or no effect on the daily lives of most of the citizens.

None of the Historical Notes are intended to have any connection with the stories I have written. They are included rather as a part of the whole picture I am presenting in my books, and to indicate that such things were, in fact, happening.

Gunplay did not enter the life of every citizen, although a time might come when any man might be called upon to defend himself. The law, if present, was often beyond call, even as now. Nor was the western man inclined to call for help. He who settled his own difficulties was most respected.

The gunfighter was not inclined to wear a gun slung low on his hip, and swagger about town. That was for the tinhorns or the would-bes. More often than not he dressed in a conservative manner and went about his business quietly and with dignity. In fact, in one of the most noted gun duels, where two of the top operators in the field met, both men drew not from low-slung holsters but from their hip pockets. This was the fight in Fort Worth between Long-Haired Jim Courtright and Luke Short.

Television and motion pictures have made everyone familiar with the names of Billy the Kid, Wild Bill Hickok, Bat Masterson, and Wyatt Earp, so I have purposely avoided them. In their time there were at least a hundred men as well, if not better, known.

Various cliches have arisen from one source or another, and one that resulted from its use in the Spanish-American War is the notion that "a .45 will always knock a man down." Don't you believe it. I could relate at least a hundred cases where men took .45-caliber bullets and kept right on coming.

Another cliche of motion pictures and television is the gunman or outlaw who, alone or with a gang, terrorizes a western town. One has to remember that the period of the gunfighter was in the years of the mining booms and cattle drives following the Civil War. Several hundred thousand men went west, from the army or civilian life, who had been using guns. Many were veterans of the Union or Confederate armies, and they not only could shoot but had been shooting. Others were veterans of Indian fighting, and a large percentage of those who came west had hunted meat for the table. They knew just as much about guns and had used them as much or more than any pack of ratty outlaws who came down the pike. And they weren't about to take any nonsense.

An illustration: In Northfield, Minnesota a bunch of farmers and businessmen shot the Jesse James gang almost out of existence, and in Coffeyville, Kansas the local citizenry wiped out the Doolin-Dalton gang. Emmett Dalton survived to sell real estate in Los Angeles, but he was carried from the field pretty well ballasted with buckshot. One could list a dozen more such occasions.

All this was but one aspect of a varied picture, for most people worked hard and for long hours. Social activity for families and many others centered around the churches, although there were dances, box suppers, horse races, as well as foot races (a very popular activity), and some towns such as Dodge City had both band concerts and baseball games. Often there were prize fights. Occasionally traveling groups of actors would present their shows.

Court sessions were eagerly awaited for the drama they offered, and certain trial lawyers had greater followings than any matinee idol. The same was true of revival ministers who preached the gospel in small western towns. Many of those in the audience came more to hear his presentation than for the Holy Word, a fact of which he was usually aware.

BUCKSKIN RUN

THE GHOSTS OF
BUCKSKIN RUN

For two days they had seen no other traveler, not even a solitary cowhand or an Indian. There had been the usual stops to change teams, an overnight layover at Weston's ranch, but no other break in the monotony of the journey.

There was no comfort in the west-bound stage. The four passengers alternately dozed or stared miserably at the unchanging desert, dancing with heat waves.

No breeze sent a shaft of coolness through the afternoon's heavy heat. Aloma Day, bound for Cordova, a tiny cowtown thirty miles further along the trail, felt stifled and unhappy. Her heavy dress was hot, and she knew her hair "looked a fright."

The jolting of the heavy coach bouncing over the rocky, ungraded road had settled a thin mantle of dust over her clothes and skin. The handkerchief with which she occasionally touched her cheeks and brow had long since become merely a miserable wad of damp cloth.

Across from her Em Shipton, proprietor of Cordova's rooming and boarding establishment, perspired, fanned, and dozed. Occasionally she glanced with exasperation at Aloma's trim figure, for to her the girl seemed unreasonably cool and immaculate. Em Shipton resembled a barrel with ruffles.

Mark Brewer, cattle buyer, touched his mustache thoughtfully and looked again at the girl in the opposite corner of the stage. She was, he decided, almost beautiful. Possibly her mouth was a trifle wide, but her lips were lovely, and she laughed easily.

"I hope," he ventured suddenly, "you decide to stay with us, Miss Day. I am sure the people of Cordova will do all they can to make your visit comfortable."

"Oh, but I shall stay! I am going to make my home there."

"Oh? You have relatives there?"

"No," she smiled, "I am to be married there."

The smile left his eyes, yet hovered politely about his lips. "I see. No doubt I know the lucky fellow. Cordova is not a large town."

Loma hesitated. The assurance with which she decided upon this trip had faded with the miles. It had been a long time since she had seen Rod Morgan, and the least she could have done was to await a reply from him. Yet there was no place in which to wait. Her aunt had died, and they had no friends in Richmond. She had money now for the trip. Six weeks or a month later she might have used it all. Her decision had been instantly made, but the closer she came to Cordova the more uncertain she felt.

She looked at Brewer. "Then you probably know him. His name is Roderick Morgan."

Em Shipton stiffened, and Mark Brewer's lips tightened. They exchanged a quick, astonished glance. Alarmed at their reaction, Loma glanced quickly from one to the other.

"What's the matter? Is something wrong?"

"Wrong?" Em Shipton had never been tactful. "I should say there is! Rod Morgan is an insufferable person! What can you be thinking of to come all this way to marry a man like that?"

"Please, Em," Brewer interrupted. "Remember, you are speaking of Miss Day's fiancé. Of course, I must admit it is something of a shock. How long since you have seen him, Miss Day?"

"Two years." She felt faint, frightened. What was wrong? What had Rod done? Why did they—

All through her aunt's long illness, Rod's love for her had been the rock to which she clung, it had been the one solid thing in a crumbling world. He had always been the one to whom she knew she could turn.

"That explains it, then," Brewer said, sympathetically. "A lot can happen in two years. You haven't been told, I presume, of the murders in Buckskin Run?"

"No. What is Buckskin Run?"

"It's a stream, you know. Locally, it is the term used to designate the canyon through which the stream runs, as well as the stream itself. The stream is clear and cold, and it heads far back in the mountains, but the canyon is rather a strange, mysterious sort of place, which all decent people avoid like the plague. For years the place has been considered haunted, and there are unexplained graves in the canyon. Men have died there under unexplained circumstances. Then Rod Morgan moved into the canyon and built a cabin there."

"You—you spoke of murders?"

"Yes, I certainly did. About a year ago Morgan had trouble with a man named Ad Tolbert. A few days later a cowhand found Tolbert's body not far from Morgan's cabin. He had been shot in the back."

"And that was only one of them!" Em Shipton declared. "Tell her about the pack peddler."

"His name was Ned Weisl. He was a harmless old fellow who had been peddling around the country for years. On every trip he went into Buckskin Run, and that seemed strange, because until Morgan moved there nobody lived in the Run country. He had some wild story he told about gold in Buckskin Run, some gold buried there. About a month ago they found his body, too. And he had been shot in the back."

"You mark my words!" Em Shipton declared. "That Rod Morgan's behind it all!"

The fourth passenger, a bearded man, spoke for the first time, "It appears to me that you're condemning this young man without much reason. Has anybody seen him shoot anybody?"

"Who would go into that awful place? Everybody knows it's haunted. We warned young Morgan about it, but he was too smart, a know-it-all. He said all the talk about ghosts was silly, and even if there were ghosts he'd make them feel at home!

"We thought it was strange, him going into that dark, lonely place! No wonder. He's deep, he is! With a sight of crime behind him, too!"

"That's not true!" Loma said. "I've known Rod Morgan for years. There isn't a nicer boy anywhere."

Em Shipton's features stiffened with anger. A dictator in her own little world, she resented any contradiction of her opinions.

"I reckon, young lady, you've a lot to learn, and you'll learn it soon, mark my words!"

"There is something to what Mrs. Shipton says," Brewer commented. "Morgan does have a bad reputation around Cordova. He was offered a good riding job by Henry Childs when he first arrived, but he refused it. Childs is a pioneer, and the wealthiest and most respected man in the country. When a drifter like Morgan refused such a job it aroused suspicion. Why would a man want to live in that canyon alone, when he could have a good job with Childs?"

"Maybe he simply wants to be independent. Maybe he wants to build his own ranch," the bearded man suggested. "A man never gets anywhere working for the other man."

Mark Brewer ignored the comment. "That canyon has always had an evil reputation. Vanishing wagon trains, mysterious deaths, and even the Indians avoid the place."

He paused. "You've only one life to live, Miss Day, so why don't you wait a few days and make some inquiries before you commit yourself? After all, you do admit you haven't seen the man for two years."

Aloma Day stared out over the desert. She was angry, but she was frightened, also. What was she getting into? She knew Rod, but two years is a long time, and people change. So much could have happened.

He had gone west to earn money so they could be married, and it seemed unlikely he would think of building a home for her in a haunted valley. He was, she knew, inclined to be hot-headed and impulsive.

But *murder*? How could she believe that of him?

"It doesn't make a man a murderer because he lives in a nice little valley like Buckskin Run," the bearded man said. "You make your inquiries, ma'am, that's a sensible suggestion, but don't take nobody's word on a man on evidence like that. Buckskin Run is a pretty little valley."

Mark Brewer gave the man his full attention for the first time. "What do you know about Buckskin Run? Everybody agrees it's a dangerous place."

"Nonsense! I've been through it more than once. I went through that valley years ago, before your man Childs was even out here.

"Pioneer, is he? I never heard of him. There wasn't a ranch in the country when I first rode in here. As far as Indians are concerned, Buckskin Run was medicine ground. That's why they never went there."

"How do you explain the things that have happened there?"

"I don't explain 'em. There's been killings all over the west, and will be as long as there's bad men left. There were white men around when I first came in here, renegades most of 'em, but nobody ever heard any talk of haunts or the like. Men like Tarran Kopp camped in there many's the time!"

"You were here," Brewer asked, "when Tarran Kopp was around?"

"Knowed him well. I was through this here country before he ever seen it. Came through with Kit Carson the first time, and he was the one named it Buckskin Run. Favorite camp ground for Kit, that's what it was.

"My name's Jed Blue, and my feet made trails all over this country. I don't know this man Morgan, but if he's had the sense to settle in Buckskin Run he's smart. That's the best growing land around here!"

Em Shipton glared at Jed Blue. "A lot you know about it! That valley is a wicked place! It's haunted, and everybody from Cordova to Santa Fe knows it. What about the wagon trains that went into it and disappeared?

"What about the graves? Three men buried side by each, and what does it say on their markers? 'No visible cause of death on these bodies.' "

The Concord rumbled through a dry wash, then mounted the opposite bank with a jerk, bumped over a rock in the trail, and slowed to climb a steep, winding grade.

Talk died as suddenly as it had begun, and Loma clenched

her hands in her lap, fighting back the wave of panic that mounted within her.

If Rod had become what they said, what would she do? What *could* she do? Her money was almost gone, and she would be fortunate if she had enough to last a week. Yet, what would have happened had she remained in the East? To be without money in one place was as bad as another.

Yet, despite the assurance with which they spoke, she could not believe Rod was a murderer. Remembering his fine, clean-cut face, his clear, dark eyes, and his flashing smile, she could not accept what they said.

The Concord groaned to the top of the grade, and the six horses swung wide around a curve and straightened out, running faster and faster.

Suddenly there was a shot, a sharp yell, and the stage made a swerving stop so abruptly that Loma was thrown into Em Shipton's lap. Recovering, she peered out of the window.

A man lay flat in the middle of the trail, blood staining the back of his vest. Beside his right hand lay a six-shooter.

To the left of the road were four riders, sitting their horses with hands uplifted. Facing the four from the right side of the road was a young man with dark, wavy hair blowing in the wind. He wore badly worn jeans, scuffed star boots and a black and white checkered shirt. There was an empty holster on his hip, and he held two guns in his hands.

"Now pick up your man and get out of here! You came hunting it, and you found it."

Loma stifled a cry. "Rod!" she gasped. "Rod Morgan!"

Her voice was low, but Jed Blue overheard. "Is that your man?" he asked.

She nodded, unable to speak. It was true then, she thought. He *was* a killer! He had just shot that man.

One of the horsemen caught the riderless horse and two of the others dismounted to load the body across the saddle. The other man sat very still, holding his hand on the pommel of his saddle.

As the other riders remounted he said, "Well, this is one you won't bury in Buckskin Run!"

"Get going!" Morgan said. "And keep a civil tongue in your

head, Jeff. I've no use for you or any of your rustling, dry-gulching crowd."

Loma Day drew back into the stage, her hands to her face. Horror filled her being. That limp, still body! Rod Morgan had killed him!

"Well!" Em Shipton said triumphantly. "What did we tell you?"

"It's too bad you had to see this," Brewer said. "I'm sorry, ma'am."

"That's a right handy young feller!" Blue said admiringly. "Looks to me like you picked you a good one, ma'am. Stood off the five of them, he did, and I never seen it done better. Any one of them would have killed him had they the chance, but he didn't even disarm them. And they wanted no part of him!"

The stage started to roll.

"Hey?" Blue caught at Loma's arm. "Ain't you even goin' to call to him? Ain't you goin' to let him know you're here?"

"No! Don't tell him! Please, don't!"

Blue leaned back, shaking his head admiringly. "Handy, right handy! That gent who was down in the road was drilled plumb center!"

Loma did not hear him. Rod! Her Rod! A *killer*!

As the stage swung back into the road and pulled away, Rod Morgan stooped and picked up the dead man's six-shooter. No use wasting a good gun, and if things went on as they had begun he would have need of it.

He walked back to where his gray mustang was tethered, and swung into the saddle. A brief glance around and he started back up the canyon. There was so much to do, and so little time.

Perhaps he had been wrong to oppose the ingrained super-stition and suspicion of the Cordova country, but working as a cowhand would never allow him to save enough to support a wife or build a home. Buckskin Run, from the moment he had first glimpsed it, had seemed the epitome of all he had dreamed.

The stream plunged happily over the stones, falling in a series of miniature cascades and rapids into a wide basin surrounded by towering cliffs. It flowed out of that basin and through a wide meadow, several hundred acres of good grassland. High cliffs bordered the area on all sides, and there were clumps of aspen and spruce.

Below the first meadow lay a long valley also bounded by sheer cliffs, a valley at least a half-mile wide that narrowed suddenly into a bottleneck that spilled the stream into another series of small rapids before it swung into the timbered land bordering the desert.

When Rod Morgan had found Buckskin Run there had been no tracks of either cattle or horses. Without asking questions, he chose a cabin site near the entrance and went to work. Before he rode out to Cordova on his first trip to town his cabin was built, his corrals ready.

In Cordova he ran into trouble with Em Shipton.

Em's entire life was ruled by prejudice and superstition. She had come to Cordova from the hills of West Virginia by way of Council Bluffs and Santa Fe. In the Iowa town she married Josh Shipton, a teamster freighting over the Santa Fe Trail. She had already been a widow, her first husband dropping from sight after a blast of gun-fire with his brother-in-law.

Josh Shipton was more enduring, and also somewhat faster with a gun, than Em's previous spouse. He stood her nagging and suspicion for three months, stood the borrowing and drunkenness of her brother for a few days longer. The two difficulties came to a head simultaneously. Josh packed up and left Em and, in a final dispute with her quarrelsome, pistol-ready brother, eliminated him from further interference in Em's marital or other affairs. But Josh kept on going.

Em Shipton had come to Cordova and started her rooming and boarding house while looking for a new husband. Her first choice, old Henry Childs himself, was a confirmed bachelor who came to eat once at her table. Wiser than most, he never came again.

She was fifteen years older and twenty pounds heavier than slim, handsome Rod Morgan, but he was her second choice.

"What you need," she told him, "is a good wife!"

Unaware of the direction of the conversation, Rod agreed that he did.

"Also," she said, "you must move away from that awful canyon. It's haunted!"

Rod laughed. "Sure, and I've seen no ghost, ma'am. Not a one. Never seen a prettier valley, either. No, I'm staying."

Em Shipton coupled her ignorance with assurance. Women were scarce in the West, and she had come to consider herself quite a catch. She had yet to learn that women were not *that* scarce.

"Well," she said definitely, "you can't expect me to go live in no valley like that."

Rod stared, mouth open in astonishment. "Who said anything—" He swallowed, trying to keep a straight face but failing. He stifled the laugh, but not the smile. "I'm sorry. I like living there, and, as for a wife, I've plans of my own."

Em might have forgiven the plans, but she could never forgive that single, startled instant when Rod realized that Em Shipton actually had plans for him herself, or the way he smiled at the idea.

That was only the beginning of the trouble. Rod Morgan had walked along to the Gem Saloon, had a drink, and been offered a job by Jake Sarran, Henry Childs' foreman. He refused it.

"Better take it, Morgan," Sarran advised, "if you plan to stay in this country. We don't like loose, unattached riders drifting around."

"I'm not drifting around. I own my own place on Buckskin Run."

"I know," Sarran admitted, "but nobody stays there long. Why not take a good job when you can get it?"

"Because I simply don't want a job. I'll be staying at Buckskin Run." As he turned away a thought struck him. "And you can tell whoever it is who wants me out of there that I've come to stay."

Jake Sarran put his glass down hard, but whatever he intended to say went unspoken. Rod left the saloon, his brow furrowed with thought and some worry. On this first visit to town he had come to realize that his presence at Buckskin Run was disturbing to someone.

For a week he kept busy on the ranch, then he rode south, hired a couple of hands, and drove in three hundred head of whiteface cattle. With grass and water they would not stray, and there was no better grass and water than that in Buckskin Run. He let the hands go.

But the thought worried him. Why, with all that good pasture and water, had Buckskin Run not been settled?

When next he rode into Cordova he found people avoiding him. Yet he was undisturbed. Many communities were clannish and shy about accepting strangers. Once they got acquainted it would be different. Yet he had violated one of their taboos.

It was not until he started to mount his horse that he discovered his troubles were not to stop with being ignored. A sack of flour tied behind his saddle had been cut open, and most of the flour had spilled on the ground.

Angered, he turned to face the grins of the men seated along the walk. One of them, Bob Carr, a long, rangy rider from Henry Childs's Block C, had a smudge of white near his shirt pocket, and another smudge near his right-hand pants pocket, the sort of smear that might have come from a man's knife if he had cut a flour-sack open, then shoved the knife back in his pocket.

Rod had stepped up on the walk. "How'd you get that white smudge on your pocket?"

The rider looked quickly down, then, his face flushing, he looked up. "How do you think?" he said.

Rod hit him. He threw his fist from where it was, at his belt, threw it short and hard into the long rider's solar plexus.

Bob Carr had not expected to be hit. The blow was sudden, explosive and knocked out every bit of wind he had.

"Get him, Bob!" somebody shouted, but as Bob opened his mouth to gasp for air, Rod Morgan broke his jaw with a right.

Rod Morgan turned, and mounted his horse. From the saddle he looked back. "I didn't come looking for trouble, and I am not asking for it. I'm a quiet man, minding my own affairs."

Yet when he rode out of town he knew he had opened a feud with the Block C. It was trouble he did not want, and for which he had no time, but whether he liked it or not he had a fight on his hands.

When he returned to his cabin a few days later, after checking some cattle in the upper canyon, there was a notice nailed to his door to get out and stay out. Then his cabin was set afire and much of his gear burned.

Ad Tolbert picked a fight with him and got soundly whipped, but a few days later Tolbert was murdered in Buckskin Run. Rod Morgan took to packing a gun wherever he went.

As is the case with any person who lives alone, or is different, stories were circulated about him, and he became suspect to many people who did not know him and had never so much as seen him. Behind it there seemed to be some malignant influence, but he had no idea who or what was directing it.

Two things happened at once. A letter came from Aloma Day, and Ned Weisl came into the canyon. He had hesitated to suggest that Loma come west with the situation unsettled as it was, yet from her letter he understood what her situation must be. He had written, explaining what he could and inviting her to come.

Weisl was a strange little man. Strange, yet also charming and interesting. From the first he and Rod hit it off well, and so he told Rod about the gold.

"Three men came west together," Weisl explained. "Somewhere out in Nevada they struck it rich. The story was they had a hundred and twenty thousand in gold when they started back. They built a special wagon with a false bottom in it, where they hid the gold. Then, with three wagons in all, they headed east.

"They got as far as Buckskin Run, and there, according to the story, Tarran Kopp and his gang hit them. The three men were killed, and that was the end of it, only there was another story. With gold there nearly always is.

"One of Kopp's gang was a friend of mine years later, and when asked about it he claimed they had killed nobody in Buckskin Run, nor had they stolen any gold. At the time it all took place they were in Mexico, and he showed me an old newspaper story to prove it."

"So what became of the gold? And who did kill the people in Buckskin Run?"

"Nobody knows who killed them or how. Nobody knows what became of the gold, either. A hundred and twenty thousand in gold isn't the easiest thing to carry around in a country where people are inclined to be curious. According to the prices at the time, that would be right around three hundred pounds of gold. There are people who were right interested in that gold who claim it never left Buckskin Run!

"There's others who declare nobody went into the canyon from the lower end, and nobody knows who buried the three who died there. Markers were set over the graves, and on each one those words 'No visible mark of death on these bodies.' "

"What do you think?"

"That," Weisl said, smiling with puckish humor, "is another question. I've an idea, but it's a fantastic one. You hold the land now. Will you let me look around? I will give you one-third of whatever I find."

"Make it half?"

Weisl shrugged. "Why not? There will be enough for both."

Ned Weisl did not return to the cabin, so Rod had gone looking for him. He did not distrust the little man, but he was worried.

He found Ned Weisl—dead. He had been shot in the back.

Rod Morgan knew they believed him guilty of the murder, as well as of the killing of Ad Tolbert. No one accused him, although veiled references were made. Only today, on the trail, had he been directly accused.

He had ridden through the bottleneck and down to the stage trail, intending to ask the driver to let him know when Loma arrived, although she could scarcely have had his letter by now.

The five riders had been about to enter the bottleneck. Jeff Cordell was leading, and one of the men with him was Reuben Hart, who had the name of being a bad man with a gun. He was the man Morgan watched.

"Howdy," he said.

"We're hunting strays," Cordell said. "We thought we'd come in and look you over."

"Are you asking me or telling me?"

"We're tellin' you. We don't need to ask."

"Then you've gone as far as you go. No cattle have come in here but my own. I've fenced the neck, so nothing can come in or out unless they open the gate. Any time you want a look around, just come and ask me when I'm home."

"We're going in now," Cordell said, "and if you're smart you'll stand aside."

"I'm not smart," Rod Morgan said, waiting. Inside he was on edge, poised for trouble. "I'm the kind of man who would make you ride in over at least three dead bodies. You decide if what you're doing is worth it."

Cordell hesitated. He was no fool, and Rod Morgan had already proved a surprise to both Bob Carr and Ad Tolbert. Cordell was a poker player, and Rod Morgan looked like he was holding a pat hand. He believed he could tell when a man was bluffing, and he did not believe Morgan was. He was also aware that if anybody died it was almost sure to be him.

"Let me take him." Reuben Hart shoved his horse to the fore. "I've never liked you, Morgan, and I believe you're bluffing, and I believe you're yellow!"

Reuben went for his gun as he spoke, and Reuben was a fast man.

Cordell and the others were cowhands, not gunfighters. They could handle their guns, but were not in the class of Reuben or Dally Hart.

Very quickly they realized they were not in the class of Rod Morgan, either, for he had drawn and fired so fast that his bullet hit Reuben even as that gunman's pistol cleared leather.

Reuben slid from the saddle and sprawled on the ground, and Rod Morgan was looking over his pistol at them.

Jeff Cordell noticed another thing. Morgan's gray mustang stood rock still when Morgan fired, and he knew his own bronc would not do that. Jeff Cordell put both hands on the pommel of the saddle. For a man with a horse like that and a drawn pistol, killing the rest of them would be like shooting ducks in a barrel.

The arrival of the stage saved their faces, and they loaded Hart into the saddle and headed for the home ranch.

Andy Shank expressed an opinion they were all beginning to share. "You know," Shank said, when they had ridden a couple of miles, "I believe that gent intends to stay."

Nobody said anything but Andy was not easily squelched. "Anyway," he added, "he seemed right serious about it."

But Andy had never liked Reuben Hart, anyway.

"He'll stay," Cordell's tone was grim. "Reub was never the gun-hand Dally is, and Dally will be riding to Buckskin Run."

Back on the ranch, Rod Morgan stripped the saddle from the gray and turned it into the corral. Carrying the saddle into the log barn, he threw it over a rail. Alone in the barn, he stood for a moment in the shadowed stillness.

He had killed a man.

It was not something he liked to think about. There had been no need to look his place over for strays. It was fenced at the opening and there was nowhere else a steer could get into the canyon. Nor did the Block C have any cattle running in the area. It was purely a trouble-making venture. They knew it, and so did he.

His cabin was silent. He stood inside the door and looked around. He had built well. It had four rooms, plank floors, good, solid, squared-off logs, and windows with a view.

Would Loma like it? Would she like Buckskin Run? Or would she be afraid?

Standing in the open door he looked back toward the bottle-neck, a good six hundred yards away. Green grass rolled under the slight wind, and the run, about fifty yards from the house, could be plainly heard. The high rock walls made twilight come early, but the canyon was beautiful in any light.

He closed the door and began preparing his supper. He knew what would come now, and there was nothing he could do to prevent it but run, and he would not, he could not do that. All he had was here. His hopes, his dreams, all the money he had been able to get together, all his hard work.

The people he had talked to had told him about the Harts, watching his expression as they told him. Now that he had killed Reuben, there was no way he could avoid trouble with Dally. He hoped that would end it. And it surely would, for one or both of them.

The Block C had been against him from the start, and he had no idea why. Were they always so clannish against strangers? Were they offended by his refusing a job?

His thoughts returned to his talk with Ned Weisl. He had liked the little man, but he had brought questions. Who *had* killed the three men from Nevada? What had become of their wagons? What had become of their gold? And what became of the killers themselves?

A few things he had learned. Several of the stories about him, other than those from the malicious tongue of Em Shipton, had come from the Block C, apparently from Henry Childs, a man he had never seen. He was also aware that Mark Brewer wanted him off Buckskin Run. Brewer had even gone so far as to offer him a nice little ranch some distance from the Run, and for a very reasonable price.

He fixed the barest of meals and then sat alone to eat it, thinking of Loma. Where was she now? Had she received his letter? Would she come? Dared he bring her into all this? How would she react to what happened today, for example? In the world from which she came, the killing of one man by another was a crime, and even when done in self-defense it was somehow considered reprehensible. Yet soon all that would be over, and there would be peace on Buckskin Run. Or so he hoped.

His thoughts returned to the stories. Was there gold buried here? If so, he hoped it would soon be found, so people would stop talking about it and looking for it.

When morning came again he saddled the gray and rode to the upper end of the canyon, where a dark pool of water invited the flow down from the higher mountains. He had noticed the graves there before this, but had had no time to examine them. Yet they were tangible evidence that something had happened here in Buckskin Run.

Why had Weisl been murdered? Merely to cause trouble for him? That was ridiculous. Or was the peddler dangerously close to a secret no one wanted revealed?

What fantastic idea had Weisl had, there at the end? Rod Morgan wished, desperately, that he knew. That secret might lead to the solving of the mysteries, and an end to them.

He stepped down from the gray and walked over to the three graves. Side by side, and, what he had not realized, each was marked with the name of the man who lay there. Somehow he had gotten the impression their names were unknown.

NAT TENEDOU—HARRY KIDD—JOHN COONEY

"Well? What do you make of it?"

Startled, he looked toward the voice and saw a man seated on a rock beyond the pool, a long, lean man with a red mustache. To have reached that place unheard he must have moved like a ghost. Rod was sure he had not been there when he dismounted from his horse.

"Who are you? Where did you come from?"

The man jerked a thumb back toward the cliffs. "Come down from up yonder. I always intended to have a good look at this place, but I heerd you wasn't exactly welcoming strangers."

He indicated the graves. "Knowed that Kidd. Big man. Powerful. Don't do a man no good to be strong when a bullet hits him, I reckon."

"What are you doing here?"

The man grinned slyly. "Same as you. Lookin' for that there gold. I doubt she was ever taken out of this canyon. And those wagons? Three big wagons. I seen 'em."

"You seem to know a lot about this."

"Son, them days there wasn't much went on Josh Shipton didn't know."

"Josh Shipton? You're Josh Shipton?"

"I should reckon. Never heard of another. What d'you know about Josh Shipton?"

"There's a woman in town says she was married to you."

He sprang up so suddenly he almost slipped into the pool. "*Em?* You mean Em's here? Son, don't you go tellin' folks you seen me. Especially not her! That woman would be the death of a man! Nag, nag, nag! Mornin' until night." He spat, then squinted his eyes at Rod. "She married again? That's a marryin' woman, that one."

"Not yet, but I hear she has Henry Childs in mind."

"Childs? Reckon she'd think of him. She's money-hungry, that woman is." He chuckled suddenly. "Hee, hee! I reckon that would serve ol' Henry right! It surely would!"

"Do you know him?"

Shipton's expression changed. "Me? No, I don't know him. Heard of him." Then he added, "He ain't safe to know."

"He's just a rancher, isn't he?"

Shipton shrugged. "Maybe he is, maybe he isn't. Some folks get powerful unpleasant about those who ask questions."

Nothing was to be done with Shipton present, yet Rod was sure that somewhere in the vicinity of the basin he would find a clue to the mystery of Buckskin Run. Those wagons had to have gone somewhere, and it would have taken an army of men or many teams to hoist the wagons up the cliffs. That possibility seemed out of the question.

As for the run itself, those cascades could not be negotiated by a canoe, let alone three large wagons.

Mounting up, he waved a hand at Shipton and rode away. The man was a puzzle, but obviously knew more than he was letting on. Could he have been around at the time? It was possible.

By the time he arrived at the cabin he was sure of one thing. However those wagons had escaped, they had not come down this way. The wagons, he decided, were still there, and so was the gold.

Riding up to his cabin he swung down. Only then did he see the big, bearded man seated on the bench in front of the house.

"This looks like my day for visitors. Did you come with Shipton?"

"Shipton? You don't mean Josh is around? Now that does beat all! Wait until Em hears!"

"I promised I wouldn't mention it."

"Well, I surely won't. Any man who got away from that woman deserves his freedom, believe you me."

The man stood up. "My name's Jed Blue. I'm an old timer here. Doubt if you heard of me, because I've been away for a spell. Trapped fur in this country. I come in with Carson, the first time."

"Had anything to eat?"

Blue glanced at the height of the sun. "Reckon it's gettin' on to time." He followed Morgan inside. "You've made a lot of enemies, son."

"I didn't ask for them."

"That was a neat gun job you did on Reuben Hart. Don't know's I ever saw it done better."

"You saw that? Where were you? On the stage?"

"I was. There were some other folks on it, too, including Em Shipton and a gent named Brewer. They'd been to Santa Fe, seems like." He glanced at Morgan. "There was a girl on that stage, too. Name of Loma Day."

"*Loma*? Here? But how—?"

"She said she'd come on without waiting for word from you. She had nothing back where she came from. My feelin' was she thought she'd better make the trip whilst she still had the money."

"But why didn't she say something? She must have seen me!"

Jed Blue was slicing some beef from a cold roast. "You got to think of her, and how it must've seemed. Women-folks are different than us, and she bein' from the East, and all.

"Em Shipton, she'd been tellin' her what a bad hombre you were and then she comes up when you've just killed a man.

"That killing seemed like proof of all they'd been saying about you. She's down to Cordova now, and I figured I'd better break the news so you can plan on what to do."

He paused. "She may not welcome you with open arms."

"It can't be helped. I must see her!"

"You hold on. Just think about it a mite. In the first place, she's a mighty fetchin' young woman, and that Brewer may have some ideas of his own. He's a fine-lookin' man, and one who usually gets what he wants. You'd better set down and think this through before you go in there a foggin'.

"Also, you've got to remember there will be folks expecting you now. They know this girl has come out to see you. Em Shipton will tell ever'body in town. So they may just be waitin' for you, son. You've got to think about it."

Blue was silent for a moment and then he asked, "This here Brewer, now. Does he wear a gun? D' you know anything about him?"

"I never saw him with a gun, but I've only seen him once or twice."

"I was wondering. Reminds me somewhat of a man I knew one time, a long way back."

They were eating in silence when Rod suddenly looked up.

"You didn't ride all the way out here just to tell me about Loma."

Jed Blue tipped back in his chair, his huge body dwarfing the table at which they sat. "Reckon I didn't, son. I was sort of lookin' over the lay of the land."

"In other words, you're gold hunting?"

Blue chuckled, plucking at his beard. "Right on the point, ain't you? I like that. I like a man who comes right out with it. So if I find it, what then?"

"You keep half."

Blue laughed. "You do speak out. What if I don't aim to give you none of it?"

Rod Morgan rested both hands on the table. He was not smiling. "Friend, I'm grateful for telling me my girl friend was in Cordova, but half of whatever you find is enough. The gold is on my land, but if you find it you keep half. You try to leave with all of it, and you'll have to shoot your way out."

Blue chuckled. "Of course, you might not find it so easy as with Hart. I shuck a gun pretty good myself, and I've had a bit more experience." He cut off a slice of beef and placed it between two pieces of bread. "What you going to do with your half?"

"Buy cattle, stock this place, fix it up a mite, then hire a few hands."

Blue nodded approvingly. "Canny. Makes sense. Easy money is soon gone without a sensible plan." He looked up at Rod. "Don't want a partner, do you? I'd like to work into a setup like this, and I'm a top hand, even though I don't look it."

"I'd have to think about it," Rod said. He looked at the big man again, puzzled by something he could not define. There was more to this man than there seemed on the surface, but his impression was the man would be a square shooter. "It might be a good idea," he said, "but I wouldn't take any man in with me who didn't realize what he was getting into."

"Son," Blue said, "don't you pay that no mind. I've had wool in my teeth. I'm not one to hunt trouble, but I've stood alone many's the time. When I'm pushed I can back my play. You an' me together, we could show them a thing or two."

Rod shoved back his chair. "I'm riding to town now. Want to come along?"

Jed Blue picked his teeth with a straw. He shoved back his own chair. "Don't mind if I do," he said. "I reckon I might as well get acquainted."

As they passed through the bottleneck Blue gestured off toward the open country. "There's a passel of mavericks in the canyons and draws east of here. A couple of good men could build a herd real fast."

"That's a good way to get a chance to make hair bridles. You start that and they'd have us in a rockwalled garden."

"No," Blue said seriously, "most of this stock is over a year old and unbranded. It's for anybody. A few weeks of hard work and we could make a drive, sell out, and have some working capital."

They rode in silence, Rod preoccupied with thoughts of Loma. It had been two years since he had seen her, but now that she was near he was excited, eager to see her, but worried, too. He knew now that he wanted her more than anything in life, realizing how much he had stifled thoughts of her so he could build for their future. Now that she had come west, her mind had been poisoned against him, and she had seen him kill a man without knowing anything of what came before.

Cordova lay flat and still under a baking sun. The mountains drew back disdainfully from the desert town, leaving it to fry in its own sweat and dust. A spring wagon was receiving a load of supplies in front of the general store, and a half-dozen horses stood three-legged at the hitching rail of the Gem Saloon. Jed Blue glanced over at Rod.

"More than likely she'll be at Em Shipton's. It's about the only place a decent woman can stay. Want me to ride along?"

"Wait for me at the Gem, if you can stand their whiskey."

Turning the gray toward Em Shipton's, he felt all tight inside. He dismounted, stalling a little bit, afraid of what Loma might say. All his hopes, all his dreams were bound up in her. He walked up the slatted board walk and entered the boarding house.

Loma was standing at the end of the table in what seemed to be serious conversation with Mark Brewer.

"Rod! Oh, Rod!"

Yet even as he moved toward her he saw her eyes change as they fell to his gun.

He took her hands. "It has been a long time, too long."

Suddenly she seemed uncertain, she half turned from him. "Mark? Have you met Rod Morgan?"

"No, I'm afraid not." Brewer's voice was cool, but not unfriendly. "How are you, Morgan?"

Rod nodded. She had called him Mark. "Very well, thanks." His tone sounded less cordial than he intended.

"I am surprised to see you in town," Brewer commented. "You know, I suppose, that Dally Hart is gunning for you?"

"Is he?" Loma's hands had gone cold in his. She withdrew them gently. "But that isn't unusual in Cordova, is it? Hasn't someone been gunning for me ever since I settled in Buckskin Run? And I don't mean the Harts or any of the small fry."

"Just who do you mean?"

"If I knew that I'd go call on him and ask some questions. Now would you mind leaving us alone? I'd like to talk to Loma."

Mark smiled, but there was a taunting amusement in his eyes. "Now why should I leave you alone? Miss Day is to be my wife."

Rod felt as if he had been kicked in the stomach. His eyes turned, unbelievingly, to Loma's. Her eyes fell before his. Then she looked up.

"Rod, I want you to understand. I like you ever so much, but all this killing . . . I couldn't understand it, and Mark has been so kind. I hadn't seen you, and—"

"There's nothing to explain." He was in control again. "You are as bad as the rest of them. As for you, Brewer, you've done your work well. You've taken advantage of the fact that Loma doesn't understand the West, nor the situation here. You sneaked, connived, and probably lied."

"Don't try to bully me into a shooting, Morgan! I am not even wearing a gun."

Loma was coldly furious. "Rod Morgan! To think you would dare to speak like that! Mark hasn't lied. He has been honest and sincere. He told me not to believe all they said about you, but to wait and ask. He said I should see what men like Henry Childs thought of you, and—"

"Childs? Childs, did you say? Didn't you know it was Childs and the Block C who was fighting me?"

He looked over at Brewer. "You're welcome to her, Brewer. If she can go back on one man so easily, she will go back on another."

"If I was wearing a gun—"

"What then? If you like, I'll take mine off."

"I am not a cheap brawler. You had better go now. I think you have made Miss Day unhappy enough."

Rod Morgan turned sharply away, and started for the door. Behind him he half-heard a stifled cry as if she were calling out to him, but he did not turn.

He had just reached his horse when he saw Jed Blue. Without waiting for an explanation, he turned toward him, knowing what was about to happen.

"Son," Blue spoke quietly, "Dally Hart's over there. He says he'll shoot on sight."

"Let him! I'm in the mood for it! If he wants trouble, he sure picked the right time. I'm sick of being pushed around, and if I'm to have the name of a killer I might as well pay my dues."

"Watch yourself, son!" Blue said. "There may be more than one. I'll try to cover you, but keep your eyes open."

Rod Morgan started up the street, spurs jingling as he walked. Inside he was boiling, but he knew he must steady down, for Dally Hart was a dangerous man, much more so than his brother Reuben had been. Suddenly he found himself hating everything around him. He had come to the town a friendly stranger, asking no favors of anyone, and almost from the first he had faced dislike and even hatred. Someone, he was sure, was guiding the feeling against him, disclaiming the stories yet repeating them, and that person could be he who had killed both Tolbert and Weisl.

That person might also be the one who knew where the gold was buried, knew what had happened so long ago in Buckskin Run.

But who could possibly know? How could he know? He . . . or was it she?

At that instant Rod Morgan saw Dally Hart.

The gunman had been standing behind a horse; now he stepped into the open with his back to the sun, putting the full glare in Rod's eyes.

They were over a hundred yards apart, but Rod was walking swiftly. Sights and sounds were wiped from his world, and all he could see was the slim, tall figure with the high-crowned hat standing in the middle of the street.

Vaguely, he was aware that men had come from the stores and were lining the street, oblivious of the danger of ricocheting bullets. Dust arose in little puffs as he walked, and he could feel the heat of the sun on his face. His body seemed strangely light, but each foot seemed to fall hard to the ground as he walked.

He was going to kill this man. Suddenly all the hatred, the trouble and confusion seemed to center in the slim man with the taunting, challenging eyes and the hatchet face who was awaiting him.

He was sixty yards away, forty yards. Rod saw Dally's fingers spread a little. Thirty yards. The expression on Hart's face changed; his tongue touched his lips. Rod was walking fast, closing the distance.

Twenty yards, eighteen, sixteen—

There were men, he knew, who, proud of their marksmanship, preferred distance for their shooting, but as the distance grew less and less they became aware that at short range neither man was likely to miss. Luke Short, the Dodge City gunfighter, always crowded his foes, crowded them until they lost their poise and began to back up to get distance.

Fourteen yards—

Dally Hart's nerve broke and he went for his gun. Incredibly fast, and the gun lifted in a smooth, unbroken movement. It came level and flowered with sudden flame, then his own gun bucked in his hand, and bucked again.

Dally Hart wavered, then steadied. Something was wrong with his face. His gun came up and he fired. A blow struck Morgan. His legs went weak under him, and he fired again. Hart's face seemed to turn dark, then crimson, and the gunman toppled into the dust.

From somewhere behind him a gun bellowed and as from a great distance he heard Jed Blue saying, "That was one! Who will be the next to die?"

* * *

There was a rectangle of sunlight lying inside the cabin door, and beyond it Rod could see the green, waving grass of Buckskin Run. He could hear the muted sound of the stream as it boiled over the rocks, gathering force to charge the bottleneck.

He was home, in his own cabin. He turned his head. Everything was as he had last seen it, except for one thing. There was another bed across the room, a bed carefully made up. The table was scrubbed clean, the room freshly swept. He wondered about that, wondered vaguely how long he had been here and who had brought him back.

In the midst of his wondering he fell asleep, and when he again opened his eyes it was dark beyond the door and a lamp glowed on the table. He could hear vague movements, a rustling as of garments, and he felt that if he lay still he would soon see whomever was in the room.

While he was waiting he fell asleep again, and when he awakened it was morning again and sunlight was shining through the doorway. Then he saw something else. Jed Blue was crouched near the window but well out of sight. The door was barred, and someone was moving about outside.

Rod started to lift himself up when he heard a voice he recognized as Josh Shipton's. "Halloo, in there? Anybody to home?"

Blue made no reply. It was grotesque to see the big man crouching in silence. What was he afraid of? What could Jed Blue possibly fear from Shipton? Yet it was obvious Blue did not wish to be seen.

After a while Jed Blue stood up and, standing first to one side and then to the other, peered out the window. After a careful look around, he unbarred the door. Rod hastily closed his eyes, then, after a bit, stirred on the bed and simulated awakening. When he opened his eyes the big, bearded man was standing over him.

"Coming out of it, are you?"

"What happened?"

"You killed Dally Hart, but he got two bullets into you. I

was almighty busy for a few minutes, and had to pack you out of town before I could patch you up. You lost a sight of blood, and the trip back here didn't do you any good."

"You were in it, too, weren't you? I thought I heard you shoot."

"That Block C coyote Bob Carr tried to shoot you in the back. After he went down I had to hold a gun on the others whilst we rolled our tails out of town."

"How long have I been here?"

"A week or so. You were in a bad way."

"Any other trouble?"

"Some. Jake Sarran, that Block C ramrod, rode in here with a dozen hands. Said as soon as you could ride you were to get out, and they weren't warning you again."

"To Hell with that! I'm staying."

"Want a partner? My offer still stands."

"Why not? We're cut from the same leather, I think."

Rod was silent. He wanted to ask about Loma, but was ashamed to. He waited, hoping Blue would offer some hint as to what had happened to her. Was she married? Rod sighed, trying not to think of her. After all, she had thrown him over for Mark Brewer. Still, he had to make allowances. After all, she hadn't seen him in two years, then to hear nothing but bad about him, and then to see him kill another man—

His thoughts shifted to the vanished wagons and the gold, then to the strange actions of Jed Blue when Shipton came around.

Why had Blue not wished to be seen by Josh Shipton? Or had there been others outside, and Josh simply the bait to draw him out to be killed? It was possible.

Despite his curiosity he had no doubt there was a sensible explanation, and had no doubts about his new partner. After all, the man had saved his life, had gotten him out of town when they would certainly have either killed him or let him die. Few men would dare challenge the power of the Block C, and from the memory of the horses he had seen he knew the Block C had been out in force.

Lying there through the long day he tried to find an answer for the Block C's enmity for him; so much hatred could not stem from his original fight with Carr, nor even the shooting of Reuben Hart, which had been forced on him.

Behind it there had to be a reason, and he had a hunch the trouble stemmed from the man he had never seen—Henry Childs himself.

Hour after hour, as he lay in bed, he tried to find answers to the problem of the gold and the wagons. Three men had died and been buried, three wagons had vanished along with much gold and gear. It was not until the last day he was in bed that the idea came to him, an idea so fantastic that at first he could not believe it could be possible; yet the more he considered it, the more it seemed the only possible solution.

He was recovering rapidly, and when he could sit outside in the sun, even walk a little by favoring his bad leg, he could see many evidences of Jed Blue's work. Certainly the big man did not intend just to come along for the ride.

A comfortable bench had been built, encircling a large tree close to the house, a shady, comfortable place in which to sit. A new workbench stood near the log barn, and a parapet of stones had been built, fastened with some home-made mortar. This parapet faced the canyon entrance, and had loopholes for firing. It had been built, however, so it could not be used by anyone attacking the house, for a rifleman from the house could command both sides of it, because of the angle at which it was built.

A water-barrel had been moved into the house and kept full. Several steers had been slaughtered, and the meat jerked. It was hung up inside the house. Every precaution had been taken for a full-scale siege, if it came to that.

On a shelf near the door were several boxes of pistol and rifle ammunition. Obviously, Blue had been to town, so he must know what had become of Loma.

On the fourth day on which Rod could be outside he saddled the gray and, getting a steel hook from the odds and ends on the workbench in the blacksmith shop, he took an extra length of rope and rode up the canyon toward the basin. Blue had left early and Rod had talked with him but a few minutes. He supposed the other man had ridden to town, but Jed had said nothing about his destination.

Rod was quite sure he knew now what had become of the vanished wagons. Come what may, in the next few hours he would know for sure.

He understood something else. Both Weisl and Tolbert had been killed in the canyon, and both apparently after arriving at a solution or coming close to it. He would have to be very, very careful!

Rod Morgan's sudden appearance at Em Shipton's had startled and upset Loma. Try as she might, she could not get his face from her mind, nor the hurt expression on his face when Mark told him she was to marry him, Mark Brewer.

She had been standing in the boarding house when she heard the shots, and she had rushed to the door, panic-stricken that Rod might have been killed or hurt. Mark Brewer caught her arm and stopped her.

"Better not go out! You might be killed! It is always the innocent ones who are hurt, and it is probably just Rod Morgan killing somebody else."

He had drawn her to him and kissed her lightly before turning to the door. She learned two things in that instant. She did not like to be kissed by Mark Brewer, and he had lied. He *was* carrying a gun. He was carrying it in a shoulder holster, for it pressed against her when she was in his arms.

She knew all about shoulder holsters because her uncle had been a plainclothes detective at a time when they were first beginning to be used in the East. She had not seen one since coming west.

Why had he lied? Was he afraid of Rod? Or did he merely wish to avoid trouble? Yet the lie worried her. There seemed to be something underhanded about that gun, for she had heard several times that Mark Brewer never wore a gun. Apparently no one believed he wore a gun, yet certainly he did.

The thought rankled as the days went by. She heard that Rod had killed Dally Hart and Jed Blue had killed Bob Carr. It was not until the third day that she heard that Rod Morgan had been seriously wounded and that Jed Blue had carried him out of town.

He might be dead! Horrified, she for the first time considered her own situation. She knew none of these people. Rod she had known for a long time. He had always been a gentleman and a fine man. Could he change so quickly? Or was something else happening here of which she knew nothing?

Coming downstairs from her room at Em Shipton's, she heard Rod's name mentioned in the dining room and stopped on the steps.

The voice was that of Jeff Cordell, whom she knew as one of the four men who had faced Rod that day beside the stage.

"Got to hand it to him," Cordell was saying. "Morgan has plenty of nerve, and I've never seen a faster hand with a gun. Why, that day on the trail he could have got me sure as shootin' if I'd moved a hand. I'd lay odds he'd have gotten three or maybe all of us."

"Speaking of fast hands," said another voice, "what about that Jed Blue?"

"He's good, all right. Bob Carr never knew what hit him. You know, that Blue puzzles me. Where did he come from? Why did he tie in with Morgan? He claims he was in here with Kit Carson, but I know the name of every one who ever rode with Kit, and none of them was named Blue."

Somebody laughed. "You always use the same name, Jeff? I doubt if Childs has a single rider who uses his real name. Hell, we've all had our ups and downs."

"What will come of it, Jeff?" asked the other voice.

"Morgan will be killed. You can't beat Childs. If he doesn't want a man in the country, he doesn't stay. Jed Blue will get it, too."

"Why? What's his idea?"

"Don't try. Don't even think about it. You're getting twice a regular cowhand's wages, so just do what you're told and keep your trap shut. Childs knows why, and Brewer knows. Personally, I think the two of them are land-hungry. This is good country, and they want to control it. Can't blame 'em for that."

Aloma had gone on to her room, and after she undressed and got into bed she could not sleep. What she had overheard disturbed her. There *was* a plot against Rod Morgan, just as Rod had implied. Childs *did* want him killed.

Why, Henry Childs was the wealthiest rancher anywhere around! Why would he be involved in such things? Mark Brewer and Em Shipton both spoke so highly of him, but on the other hand, who was it who gave her the first doubts about Rod? It had been Em Shipton and Mark Brewer.

Loma Day decided she must talk to Jed Blue. She recalled that he had defended Rod that day on the stage. Had he known him then? No . . . he had not. She remembered his comments at the time she recognized Rod.

It was the next day she saw Henry Childs for the first time.

She was talking to Jeff Cordell, for after overhearing the conversation in the dining room she had decided she must cultivate him and learn what he knew.

"Did you ever kill a man, Jeff?"

He looked at her quickly. "Why, I reckon I have, ma'am. I suppose there are a good many of us who have killed a man or two, not that we want to or are looking for it. These are rough times, ma'am, and a man can't always look to the law to defend him. He has to do it himself. Out here the law expects a man to do just that."

"How about that day on the trail when Rod Morgan killed Reuben Hart?"

Jeff gave her a sharp look. He knew enough of the gossip to know Loma had come west to marry Morgan. He also knew that now Mark Brewer was riding herd on the girl. He had his own opinion of Brewer, and it was not flattering. Jeff Cordell had rustled a few head here and there, and occasionally stood a stage on its ear for drinking money, but he had a wholesome respect for a decent woman.

"Ma'am, there's some would have my hide for saying this, but you asked an honest question, and you'll get an honest answer. If Rod Morgan had been a mite slower to shoot that day, he would have been killed. Reuben Hart was sent out there to kill him."

"Sent? By whom?"

Jeff Cordell had talked all he planned to. He was turning to leave when the door opened and a big man with white hair came into the room. He glanced at Jeff and then at her.

"Cordell," he said sharply, "they need you at the ranch."

"Yes, sir. I was just leaving."

He tipped his hat and walked quickly away. Loma knew instinctively that this was Henry Childs. He was not a bit as she had expected. He was a big, kindly-looking man with white hair and gray eyes. His mouth was unusually small and his lips thin, but he was a handsome man.

Cordell turned at the door. "Boss?"

Childs turned sharply, impatience showing in every line of his face. "Cordell, I—"

"Boss, I found out who that other man was. The one we saw the other day. His handle is Josh Shipton."

Loma's eyes were on Childs, and she was shocked by the change. His mouth started to open, his features stiffened, and for a moment she thought he was about to have a stroke.

Childs seemed no longer aware of her presence. For an instant his face became cruel and harsh. "Jeff, tell Mark I want to see him. Find him now, and tell him. *Now*, do you hear?"

Em Shipton bustled into the room. "Did I hear somebody use the name of Shipton?"

"Yes," Loma said as Childs left, "it was Jeff Cordell. He said he'd seen a man named Josh Shipton."

"Why, that no-account blatherskite! I thought he was dead! If I get my hands on him, I'll—!"

She left the room suddenly, breaking off in mid-sentence.

Loma went out to the wide porch and sat in one of the rockers, spreading her skirt carefully. Too many things were happening too suddenly; there were too many tangled threads and too much that demanded explanation. Whatever else Cordell might be, she felt he was being honest with her, and she now doubted that any of the others were.

She must somehow arrange to talk to Jed Blue. That he had been to town several times since Morgan had killed Dally Hart, she knew. From where she sat she could see him if he returned to town today, and she meant to be ready.

She had been a fool to let Rod go away thinking she was promised to Mark Brewer. He had proposed, but she had not accepted. She had simply told him she needed time, that everything was so mixed up, that he would have to wait.

Fortunately, it cost little to room and board at Em Shipton's, and she had a little money left. Not enough to go home, but enough to go on to Denver. She had considered that, but nothing could make her forget Rod.

It was two days later that she saw him ride into town. He always avoided the Gem Saloon, where he might run into enemies, going straight to the supply store and buying what he needed. She was becoming sufficiently attuned to western life to see that he was always careful before entering or leaving a building. Now she saw him come out of the store and start for his horse.

No one was about, so she arose, walking down the trail toward the old well, where she occasionally went. Once out of sight of the boarding house, she caught up her skirt to keep from tripping and ran down the path. Panting and somewhat disheveled, she arrived at the trail edge just as he appeared.

She stepped into plain sight and waited until he rode up to her. "Mr. Blue? I must talk to you."

"Are you alone?"

"Yes."

He glanced around quickly, then walked his horse into the bushes across the trail, and she followed. She was surprised to find a small, rustic footbridge across the creek, and an old millpond, the mill no longer in use.

Quickly, she told him what she had learned, even Childs's shock on hearing of Josh Shipton. Blue chuckled grimly at that, and then she told him of Cordell's certainty that Rod would be killed.

"Mr. Blue, how is Rod? Oh, I wish I had it all to do over! I was such a fool! But it was all so different from what I'd known. I just wish I had listened to what you said on the stage."

"Rod's coming along all right, ma'am. I'm just afraid this trouble's all coming to a head before we're ready for it.

"You say that when Childs heard about Shipton he sent for Brewer? Now what do you know about that?"

"What's wrong?"

"Ma'am, you had better keep clear of Mark Brewer. As long as you know so much you'd better know this, too. Somebody has been doin' Childs' killin' for him, and I know he wants Shipton dead, so who does he send for? Mark Brewer!"

"Oh, no! You must be mistaken!" Even as she said it she remembered the gun. "Mr. Blue, I do know this, when he told Rod that he didn't carry a gun, he lied. He wears one in a shoulder holster."

Blue was pleased. "Now, then, ma'am, that's the best news you've given me so far. That little item might save my life or Rod's."

"Why should Mr. Childs want Josh Shipton killed?"

Jed Blue hesitated. "There's the question behind this whole affair. Only two men know what happened in Buckskin Run when that gold vanished. One of them was Henry Childs; the other one is Josh Shipton."

He smiled widely. "Trouble is, for them at least, that a third one has figured it out, and I'm the third.

"Ma'am, you go back and tell them you met a man on the road, and don't describe me, who told you to tell them that Tarran Kopp is back."

She was seated in the small sitting room at the boarding house when Mark Brewer came in. Before she could speak he went on up to his room, and when he returned he was dressed for the trail. He walked over and sat down beside her.

"I hear you met Henry Childs. Quite a fellow, isn't he?"

"He's big," she admitted, "and a fine-looking man." Then, giving her face a puzzled expression, she asked, "Mark, who is Tarran Kopp?"

If she had expected a reaction she was not disappointed. He started as if stung, grabbing her wrist in a grip that hurt. "Who? Where did you hear that name?"

"Please don't! You're hurting me!" She rubbed her wrist as he released it. "Why, it was nothing at all!" She spoke carelessly. "I get so restless here, so I took a walk over by that old mill, it is so quiet and peaceful there, and I met a man. He was very polite.

"Actually, he was just watering his horse there at the millpond, and he asked me if I wasn't living at Em Shipton's. I told him I was, and he asked me to tell Henry Childs that Tarran Kopp was back."

Mark Brewer got to his feet. "He said Kopp was back? What did he look like?"

"Oh, he was just a man. As tall as you, I think, but spare. He was riding a black horse." The horse Jed Blue had been riding was a blue roan.

"This changes everything," Brewer muttered, talking more to himself than her.

"Who is Tarran Kopp? What is he?"

"Oh, he was just an outlaw who was active out here fifteen or twenty years ago. It's believed he was the one who robbed those wagons you've heard about."

He turned toward the door. "Look, if Henry Childs comes in, tell him what you just told me, will you? And tell him I need to see him."

Before noon, Rod Morgan reached the basin. After lying among the rocks for about twenty minutes while studying the terrain to be sure he was unobserved, he went down to the edge of the pool and, putting his rifle down beside him, he began to cast with the heavy iron hook. He would cast the hook as far out as possible, let it sink to the bottom, and slowly drag it back to him.

He worked steadily, tirelessly, taking occasional breaks to study the country around. He was well into his third hour, without finding anything but broken branches or moss, when the hook snagged on something. Twice it slid off before it held, and then hand over hand he drew in his catch.

A wagon tire!

An iron wagon tire, showing evidence of having been subjected to heat. So then, they must have burned the wagons, thrown the metal parts into the pool, and . . . what about the gold?

He was squatting beside the wagon tire when he heard the sharp, ugly bark of a rifle.

He hit the ground in a dive from his squat, grabbed his rifle, and rolled over behind a rock. He was lying, waiting for another shot, when he realized the bullet had come nowhere near him.

Starting to lift his head he heard two more shots, quick, sharp, fired only a breath apart.

Stones rattled, a larger one plopped into the basin, and then Rod caught a fleeting glimpse of a man's body falling. There was a terrific splash, and the body sank from sight.

Peering up, he saw a shadowy outline, a man's figure, atop the cliff, peering down. Then the shadow disappeared and, jerking off his boots and gunbelt, Morgan went into the water. Its icy chill wrenched a gasp from his throat, and then he saw the body, only it was not merely a body but a man, still struggling to live.

Diving low, he slipped an arm around the man's body and struck out for the surface. It was a struggle to get him to the surface and out upon the shore, and the man was bleeding badly.

It was Josh Shipton, and one look at the wound in his side and Rod knew there was no chance.

Shipton's lids fluttered. "B—Brew—Brewer dry-gul—dry-gulched me." He waved a feeble arm. "Childs—gold—Childs." He seemed to be trying to point toward the graves; or was it only one grave?

Brewer had killed him, but what had he been trying to say? At what had he pointed? Or was it only a wild gesture from a dying man?

Horse's hoofs pounded on the sod, a racing horse. Rod wheeled, rifle ready. It was Jed Blue.

"You all right? I heard shots." Then he saw Shipton. "Ah? So Brewer got him."

"How did you know that?"

Blue explained what Loma had told him, and what she overheard. He also added the bit about Mark Brewer's shoulder holster.

"What made Childs so afraid of Shipton?"

"They were afraid of what he knew. Shipton knew all three of the men buried there, and if he saw Henry Childs he would smell a rat, and rat is right."

"What do you mean?"

"Shipton was trying to point at one of the graves. The grave of Harry Kidd."

"Kidd? Childs? Are you telling me Kidd didn't die? That there's nobody in that grave?"

"Kidd murdered the other two, cached the gold, marked the graves so people would grow superstitious about them, then left the country. Coming back later, he started a ranch and helped spread the stories about the ghosts of Buckskin Run."

"Smart," Rod admitted.

"Except for one thing. He accused the wrong man of the murders. He spread the story around that the three had been killed and the gold stolen by Tarran Kopp."

"Kopp killed a few men here and there, but all in fair fights. He never murdered a man in his life, and that story made him mad. I know, because I am Tarran Kopp."

From far down the canyon they heard a thunder of racing hoofs, a wild cry, and then a shot. Both men turned, rifles lifting.

A small black horse was coming toward them on a dead run, and they could see a girl's long hair streaming in the wind. Behind her, still some distance away, a tight group of racing horsemen.

"It's Loma!" Rod said. "And the Block C riders!"

Dropping to one knee, he opened up with his Winchester. A rider threw up his arms and dropped from his horse, and the group split, scattering out across the small plain.

The black horse swung in toward their position and was reined in. Loma slid from the horse's back into Rod's arms. The black horse wheeled and raced off a few yards, tossing its head with excitement.

"Never figured on making a stand here," Rod said. "Jed? Have you got enough ammunition?"

"Plenty. How about you?"

"The same . . . *there's one behind that spruce!*"

He fired as he spoke and the man cried out, staggering into the open where a bullet from Jed put him down.

Bullets spattered on the rocks around them, but their position in the small basin around the pool was excellent. A man could stand erect alongside the pool and still be under cover. A ring of boulders almost surrounded the pool, and a stream of them fanned out downslope from them where the attackers were.

Rod turned to Loma. "Can you fire a rifle?"

"Just give me a chance! My father taught me to shoot when I was a little girl. Only, I—I never shot a man."

"You won't get much chance here. Those boys are pretty well snuckered down now, and they aren't about to get themselves killed. Just fire a shot in that general direction once in awhile.

"Jed, I'm going to circle around and try to get whoever is leading this bunch. My guess is it will be Brewer."

"Or Childs. Don't forget him."

Rod slid back to lower ground, wormed his way through some brush, and descended into a small wash. All of this was on land he claimed, and over which he had ridden many times. He knew every inch of it.

There had been no more than eight or ten men in the original group, and at least two were out of action. Unless he was mistaken, the Block C boys had enough. Their loyalty was largely money loyalty, and nobody wants to die for a dollar, at least nobody in his right mind.

He moved swiftly and silently along the sandy bottom, his boots making no sound in the soft sand. He was rounding a boulder when he heard a voice. It was Mark Brewer.

"Think we've got 'em, Henry?"

"Got 'em? Oh, sure! We'll finish them off, send the boys home, and dig up that gold. It's high time we dug it up. Something always kept me from going after it before. Price on gold has gone up, so we'll have more money, Mark."

"You mean," Brewer's voice was so low Rod could scarcely hear, "*I'll* have more!"

Through an opening in the rocks, Rod could see them now. He saw the surprise and shock on Childs's face turn to horror as Brewer drew a gun on him.

"Very simple, Henry. I've been waiting for this chance. I'll have it all for myself, and everybody will blame Morgan and Kopp for killing you."

Childs's hand went to his holster, but it was empty. "Don't bother, Henry. I'm making it easy for you. I lifted your gun then waited until your rifle was empty. Now I'll kill you, let the boys finish off Morgan and Kopp, and I get the gold."

The two men faced each other across ten feet of green grass, cut off from view of the Block C riders by trees and boulders and over fifty yards of distance.

Childs's small mouth tightened until it was scarcely visible. He was sullen and wary. "Well," he said casually, "I guess I've had it coming. I murdered good men for that gold and never got a penny's worth of it. Now you'll murder me. Of course, we're going out together."

His hand flashed in movement, and Mark Brewer's .44 roared. Childs swayed like a tree in the wind but kept his feet. In the palm of his hand was a small derringer. He fired, and then again.

Brewer's gun was roaring, but his last bullets were kicking up sand at Childs's feet. He went to his knees, then down to his face in the bloody sand.

Childs said, "I had a hide-out gun, too, Mark. I was half expect—"

He put out a hand for support that was not there. Then he fell, sprawling on the grass. Rod hurried to him.

His eyes flared open. "You got a mighty pretty girl there, son," he said. The two-barreled derringer slipped from his fingers and he was dead. Rod stood for a moment, staring down at him.

Without the stolen money the man had done well. He had built a ranch, fine herds of cattle, earned the respect of his community, and all for nothing. The old murders had ridden him to his death.

Rod walked around the bodies and through the trees. When he got where he could see the Block C riders he lifted his rifle.

"Drop your guns, boys! The war's over! Childs and Brewer just killed each other."

Jeff Cordell dropped his gun. "Damned if they didn't have it coming." He paused. "Mind if we look?"

"Come on, but don't get any fancy notions. Too many men have died already."

The Block C riders trooped over, and stood looking down at the derringer that had slipped from his fingers.

"Mark always said he never carried a gun except when he was out in the hills like this." He stooped and flipped back

Brewer's coat to reveal the shoulder holster. "His kind always want an edge."

Cordell started to turn away. "You can take them along, Jeff. Take 'em back down to Cordova and tell them the truth."

"Why not? All right, boys, let's clean up the mess."

When they were gone, Tarran Kopp came out of the trees. Loma was with him.

"We could have buried 'em where they fell," Kopp said.

Rod shrugged. "Maybe, but I want no more ghosts in Buckskin Run."

He glanced around at Kopp. "What name are you using from now on? If we're going to be partners I'd better know."

"Jed Blue. Tarran Kopp's a legend. He's from the past; let him stay there."

They walked away together to their horses. "We'd better dig up that gold, once for all. We can buy cattle, fix up a place for you all, and I'll take the old cabin."

He glanced slyly at Rod. "You know where it is?"

"Where you'd expect to find it. Buried in the grave of Harry Kidd."

Together, they rode back down the trail to the cabin on Buckskin Run.

Jed Blue looked around at them, pointing at the cabin. "I never had no home before," he said, "but that's home. We're a-comin' home."

MRS. PAIGE

The people who built the West, like those of whom I write, were survivors. They had to be.

Fifty books could be filled with anecdotes of men, women and children who survived under seemingly impossible conditions—survived attacks by enemies, by wild animals, by terrible storms, and hunger, thirst and cold. One of these was Mrs. Paige.

In this space I do not have the room to tell all that happened to her and her family. Her father and many of her relatives were killed by Indians. Those the Indians missed at one time, they caught up with later.

Attacked on the trail, Mrs. Paige was struck repeatedly on the head, stabbed and then thrown over a cliff. She hung briefly in a tree, and then fell the rest of the way. The Indians approached the rim and threw a number of boulders at her, some of which scored direct hits. Believing her dead, the Indians rode away. Sometime later, when she returned to consciousness, the young woman began to crawl. Despite the loss of blood and the wounds she had suffered, she crawled several miles, managing occasionally to stagger a few steps.

It was southern Arizona, the heat was around 110 degrees, but she crawled on until she had to take shelter under some low-growing brush. In all, during the next few days, she traveled most of sixteen miles before she was discovered and taken to a nearby town. She had lost almost half her normal weight, her eyes were deeply sunken in her skull, her face burned almost black and the skin shrunk tight against her skull. Yet she survived for many years.

NO TROUBLE FOR THE
CACTUS KID

E ven the coyotes who prowled along the banks of the Rio
  Salado knew the Cactus Kid was in love. What else would
cause him to sing to the moon so that even the coyotes were
jealous?

The Cactus Kid was in love, and he was on his way to Aragon
to buy his girl some calico, enough red and white calico to
make a dress.

It was seventy miles to Aragon, and the dance was on Friday. This being Monday, he figured he had plenty of time.

Red and white calico for a girl with midnight in her hair and
lovelight in her eyes. Although, reflected the Cactus Kid, there
were times when that lovelight flickered into anger, as he had
cause to know. She had made up her mind that he was the only
man for her, and he agreed and was pleased at the knowledge,
yet her anger could be uncomfortable, and the Cactus Kid
liked his comfort.

The paint pony switched his tail agreeably as he cantered
down the trail, the Kid lolling in the saddle. Only a little ride
to Aragon, then back with the calico. It would take Bonita only
a little while to make a dress, a dress that would be like a
dream once she put it on.

Love, the Cactus Kid decided, was a good thing for him.
Until he rode up to Coyote Springs and met Bonita, he

41

had been homeless as a poker chip and ornery as a maverick mule.

Now look at him! He was riding for Bosque Bill Ryan's Four Staff outfit, and hadn't had a drink in two months!

Drinking, however, had never been one of his pet vices. By and large he had one vice, a knack for getting into trouble. Not that he went looking for trouble; it was simply that it had a way of happening where he was.

The Cactus Kid was five feet nine in his socks, and weighed an even one hundred and forty pounds. His hair was sandy and his eyes were green, and while not a large man it was generally agreed by the survivors that he could hit like a man fifty pounds heavier. His fighting skill had been acquired by diligent application of the art.

On this ride he anticipated no trouble. Aragon was a peaceful town. Had it been Trechado, now, or even Deer Creek . . . but they were far away and long ago, and neither town had heard the rattling of his spurs since he met Bonita . . . nor would they.

It was spring. The sun was bright and just pleasantly warm. The birds were out, and even the rabbits seemed rather to wait and watch than run. His plan was to stop the night at Red Bluff Stage Station. Scotty Ellis, his friend, was majordomo at the station now, caring for the horses and changing teams when the stages arrived. It had been a month since he had visited with Scotty, and the old man was always pleased to have visitors.

The Cactus Kid was happy with the morning and pleased with his life. He was happy that Bosque Bill had let him have a week off to do as he pleased, work being slack at the moment. Next month it would be going full blast, and every hand working sixteen hours a day or more.

The Cactus Kid didn't mind work. He was, as Bosque Bill said, a "hand." He could ride anything that wore hair and used his eighty-foot California riata with masterly skill. He enjoyed doing things he did well, and he had found few things he couldn't do well.

The saw-toothed ridge of the Tularosa mountains combed the sky for clouds, and Spot, the sorrel and white paint, bobbed his head and cocked an ear at the Cactus Kid's singing.

The miles fell easily behind and the Kid let the paint make his own pace.

They dropped into a deep canyon following a winding trail. At the bottom the two-foot wide Agua Fria babbled along over the gravel. The Kid dropped from the saddle and let Spot take his own time in drinking. Then he lowered himself to his chest and drank. He was just getting up when the creek spat sand in his face, and the report of a rifle echoed down the canyon walls.

The Cactus Kid hit his feet running, and dove to shelter behind a boulder just as a bullet knocked chips from it.

Spot, in his three years of carrying the Kid, had become accustomed to the sounds of battle and rifle shots, and in two quick bounds was himself among the rocks and trees and out of sight.

The Kid had hit the dirt behind his boulder with his Colt in his fist. His hat off, he peered from alongside the rock to see who and why. A glance was enough to tell him his Colt wasn't going to be much help, so rolling over, he got into the rocks and scrambled back to the paint. Holstering the Colt, he slid his Winchester from its scabbard. Then he waited.

His position wasn't bad. It could be no more than an hour's ride to Red Bluff Station, and he had until Friday to return with the material. Well, until Thursday, anyway. How long did it take to make a dress?

No more shots were fired, but he waited. At first he was calm, then irritated. After all, if the dry-gulcher wanted a fight why didn't he get on with it?

No shots, no sounds. The Cactus Kid removed his hat again and eased it around the boulder on a stick. Nothing happened.

The Cactus Kid, rifle ready, stepped from behind his rocks. There was no shot, nothing but the chuckling of the stream over the gravel. Disgusted, he swung into the saddle and turned his horse upstream. In a few minutes he glimpsed a boot heel.

Rifle ready, he circled warily. It was not until he drew up beside him that he saw the man was dead. He was lying flat on his face and had been shot at least twice through the head and twice through the body. Kneeling beside him, the Cactus Kid studied the situation.

One shot, which wounded the dead man, had been fired

some time before. The wounded man had crawled here, seeking shelter. He had been followed and shot at least twice more while lying on the ground.

Whoever had done the killing had intended it to be just that, a killing. This was not merely a robbery.

The dead man's pockets were turned inside out, and an empty wallet lay on the ground. Empty of money, that is. There were several papers in the wallet, a couple of faded letters and a deed. A sweat stain ran diagonally across the papers.

Pocketing them, the Cactus Kid looked around thoughtfully. Seeing some bloodstains, he followed the track left by the wounded man back to the main trail. Here the story became simple.

The man had been riding along the trail toward the canyon when shot. He had fallen from his horse into the dust, had gotten to his feet, and had fired at his killer. Two empty cartridge cases lay on the ground.

Evidently the wounded man had ejected the two empty shells and reloaded, and then had been hit again and had tried to crawl to a hiding place or a better place from which to fight.

Scouting around and checking obvious ambush sites, the Kid found where the killer had waited, smoking a dozen or more cigarettes. There were marks in the dust where a saddle had rested.

A saddle, and no horse? Scouting still more, he found the horse. It was a rangy buckskin, and from the looks of it the horse had been literally run to death. Its hair was streaked with dried sweat and foam.

"Whoever he was," the Kid said aloud, "he was goin' someplace in a hurry, or gettin' away from something. He killed his horse, then holed up here until a rider came along, dry-gulched him, robbed the body, and rode off on his horse."

Returning, the Kid rolled the dead man's body over a small sand-bank, then caved the sand over him and added rocks and brush.

Whoever had fired at him had been the killer, and he could not be far ahead. The hour was now getting close to sunset, and if the Kid wanted to join Scotty Ellis at supper he had best hurry.

The sun was over the horizon when he loped his horse down to the Red Bluff Station. Scotty came to the door shading his eyes against the last glare of sunlight.

"Kid! Sakes alive, Kid! I ain't seen you in a coon's age! Some cowhand from over at the Four Star told me you was fixin' to get yourself hitched up."

"Got it in mind, Scotty. A man can't run maverick all his life." He led his horse to the corral and stripped the gear from his back, glancing around as he did so. No strange horses in the corral, no recent tracks except for the stage, a few hours back.

He followed Scotty into the station, listening with only half his attention to the old man's talk. It was the chatter of a man much alone, trying to get it all said in minutes.

As he dished up supper the Kid asked, "Any riders come through this afternoon?"

"Riders? Yep, two, three of them went by. One big feller headin' toward Coyote Springs, and a couple more pointin' toward Aragon."

"Two? Riding together?"

"Nope. They wasn't together. A big feller on a blood bay come through, and a few minutes later another feller, almost as big, ridin' a grulla mustang. Neither of them stopped. Folks are gettin' so they don't even stop to pass the time o' day!"

Two men? He had seen only one, but if they arrived at about the same time then the other rider must have been within the sound of the rifle when the killer had fired at the Kid.

At daybreak he rolled out of his blankets, fed and watered his horse, then washed and dried his hands and face at the washbowl outside the door.

"Scotty," he asked, over his second cup of coffee, "did you get a good look at either of those riders?"

"Wal, don't recollect I did. Both big fellers. Feller on the bay hoss had him one of those ol' Mother Hubbard saddles."

Riding out for Aragon, the Kid reflected that none of it was his business. The thing to do was report what he'd found to the sheriff or his deputy in Aragon, then buy his calico and head for home.

He smiled at himself. A few weeks back, before he met Bonita, he would have been so sore at that gent who fired at him that he'd not have quit until he found him. Now he was older and wiser.

Aragon was a one-street town with a row of false-fronted buildings on one side, on the other a series of corrals. The buildings consisted of a general store, two saloons, a jail with the deputy sheriff's office in front, a boarded up Land Office and two stores.

As he rode along the street his eyes took in the horses at the hitching rail. One of them was a blood bay with a Hubbard saddle, the other a grulla. The horse with the Mother Hubbard saddle had a Henry rifle in the boot. The grulla's saddle scabbard carried an old Volcanic.

The deputy was not in his office. A cowhand sitting on the top rail of the corral called over that the deputy had ridden over to Horse Mesa. The Cactus Kid walked back along the street and entered the busiest saloon. One drink and he would be on his way. Picking up the calico would require but a few minutes.

Several men were loitering at the bar. One was a lean, wiry man with bowed legs, and a dry, saturnine expression. He glanced at the Cactus Kid and then looked away. There was another man, standing near him but obviously not with him, who was a large, bulky man with bulging blue eyes which stared at the Kid like a couple of aimed rifles.

Of course, even the Cactus Kid would have admitted that he was something to look at when not in his working clothes. He was, he cheerfully confessed, a dude. His sombrero was pure white, with a colored horsehair band. His shirt was forest green, and over it he wore a beautifully tanned buckskin vest heavily ornamented with Indian work in beads and porcupine quills. His crossed gun belts were of russet leather, the belt and holsters studded with silver. His trousers were of homespun, but striped, and his boots were highly polished, a rare thing on the frontier.

The larger of the two men eyed him disdainfully, then looked away. The Kid was used to that, for those who did not know him always assumed he was a tenderfoot, a mistake that had led to more than one bit of the trouble that seemed to await him at every corner.

The larger of the two men had several notches carved in his gun butt.

The Kid ordered his drink, but he decided he did not like the man with the bulging eyes. He had never liked anybody who carved notches in their gun butts, anyway. It was a tin-horn's trick.

The Kid looked at Joe Chance, the bartender, who was obviously uneasy, and had been so ever since the Kid walked into the saloon.

The Kid had promised Bonita not to get into trouble, but nonetheless what he had found had been a coldblooded ruth-less murder and one of the two men had done it. Both had been riding, as was obvious from the trail dust they carried, and, from the attitudes of the others in the room, both were strangers.

"Chance," he said, "what would you think of a man who dry-gulched a passing rider, then walked up and shot into him a couple of times to make sure he was dead, then took his horse?"

Joe Chance knew the Cactus Kid. The mirror he now had behind the bar had caused the Kid to cough up three months wages to pay for it, and it had only been in place about sixty days.

Chance shifted his eyes warily and reached for a glass to polish. "Why, I'd think the man was a dirty murderer who deserved hangin'!"

After a pause, his own curiosity getting the best of him, he asked, "Who done such a thing?"

"Why, I don't rightly know at this minute, but I got an idea we'll find out. He came over the trail just ahead of me. He robbed the man he murdered, and he's in town right now!"

The bow-legged man lifted his eyes to meet those of the Kid. There was something mocking and dangerous in those eyes. The Kid knew he was looking into the eyes of a man who both could and would shoot. "I just rode in," the man said calmly.

"So did I." The big man·put his glass down hard on the bar. "Are you aimin' that talk at us?"

"No," the Kid said mildly, "only at one of you. Only, the other man must have heard those shots, and I'm wondering why he didn't do anything."

"What did you do?" the bow-legged man asked.

"Nothing. The killer caught sight of me and tried to cut me down, too. Hadn't been for that I'd have ridden right on by and I'd never have seen the dead man.

"The man who was killed," he added, "went by the name of Wayne Parsons. He was from Silver City."

"Never heard of him." The biggest of the two men obviously shifted his gun. "I come from Tombstone." His eyes rested on the Cactus Kid, and their expression was anything but pleasant. "They call me the Black Bantam."

"Never heard of you," he lied. Bantam was a notorious outlaw who had been riding, it was said, with Curly Bill.

"There's plenty of people who has," Bantam said, "and if I was you, young feller, and I didn't want to get all them purty clothes bloody, I'd go herd my cows and leave my betters alone."

"I didn't come to town huntin' sheep," the Cactus Kid said calmly, "or I'd dig my hands in your wool. Nor did I come for cows. I came to get some calico for my girl's dress, which doesn't leave me much time to curry your wool, Bantam.

"All I've got to say is that one of you is riding a dead man's horse and carryin' stolen money."

Bantam's fury was obvious. He was facing the bar, but he turned slowly to face the Kid. Men backed off to corners of the room, and the bartender took a tentative step toward them, then changed his mind and backed off. "Now, see here—!" he started to say, when—

"Hold it, Bantam!"

All heads turned at the interruption. It was the bow-legged rider. "Nobody's asked me who I am, and I'm not plannin' to explain. If you need a handle for me just call me Texas.

"But Bantam it seems to me this is between us. He says one of us is guilty, so why don't we settle this between us? Just you and me?" Texas smiled. "Besides, I don't think you'd like takin' a whippin' from that youngster."

"Whuppin'? Why, I'd—!"

"No, you wouldn't, Bantam. I've known all about you for a long time, and you never did hunt trouble with anybody who'd have a chance. This dude youngster here is the Cactus Kid.

"Now it seems to me it is between us, so why don't we just empty our pockets on the table here so everybody can see what we're carrying.

"The Kid is handy at readin' sign, so maybe he will see something that will tell him which one of us is the killer." He moved closer, his eyes dancing with a taunting amusement. "How about it, Kid?"

The Kid's eyes shifted from one to the other, the one taunting and challenging, the other stubborn and angry.

"Why not?" Bantam thrust a big hand into his pocket and began putting the contents of his pockets on the table. The man who called himself Texas did likewise.

"There it is, Kid. Look it over!"

Joe Chance leaned over the bar to watch, as did Slim Reynolds and Art Vertrees, the only others present.

In the pile Texas made were a worn tobacco pouch, a jackknife, a plug of chewing tobacco, several coins, a small coil of rawhide string, and a small handful of gold coins wrapped in paper. There were two rifle bullets.

In Bantam's pile there was a wad of paper money, some sixty dollars worth, some small change, a Mexican silver peso, a jackknife, a plug of chewing tobacco, a stub pipe, a tight ball of paper, a comb, and some matches.

Thoughtfully, the Cactus Kid looked over the two piles. There was nothing that could be identified with any man. It was merely such stuff as could be found in the pockets of any cowhand. Except—he picked up the ball of tightly rolled paper and slowly unrolled it.

It unfolded into a plain sheet of writing paper that had been folded just once. There were also marks that made it appear the paper had been folded about something. The crinkling from being rolled up was obviously more recent than the soiled line of the old crease.

It was not the fold the Kid was noticing, nor the faint imprint of what might have been carried within that folded sheet but rather the diagonal line of the sweat stain that ran across the papers.

"That ain't mine!" Bantam protested. "I had no such paper in my pocket!" He was suddenly frightened and his lips worked nervously. "I tell you—!"

Texas had drawn back to one side, poised and ready.

The Cactus Kid drew the dead man's papers from his pocket and placed them beside the folded paper. The diagonal sweat stains matched perfectly.

"So?" Texas said. "It was you, Bantam! You killed him!"

"You're a liar!" Bantam said angrily. "I done no—!"

Texas' hand streaked for his gun, and Bantam grabbed at his own gun. The two shots sounded almost as one, but it was Bantam who fell.

Texas holstered his gun. "Had no idea he'd draw on me, but a man's got to watch those kind."

Nobody replied, and he gathered his things from the bar and went outside.

The Kid turned back to Joe Chance. "Better give me another shot of rye; then I'm picking up my calico and headin' for home. This town's too sudden for me."

Two of the bystanders took the big man's body out, and later Slim Reynolds came in. "He must have cached that stolen money somewhere because he surely didn't have it on him."

"Bantam's had it coming for a long time," Vertrees said, "and Texas was right. He never killed anybody in a fair fight."

"What about that grulla mustang of his?" Reynolds asked. "That's a mighty fine horse."

The Kid put his glass down on the bar. "Did Bantam ride the grulla? Are you sure?"

"Of course," Vertrees replied, surprised. "I was on the street when he rode in. He was only a little ahead of Texas, who was riding a bay."

The Cactus Kid turned and started for the door. He was in the saddle and started down the street when he thought of the calico.

Bonita wouldn't like this. He had promised her faithfully he'd return with that calico, and after all, hunting killers was

the sheriff's job. Angrily, he turned the paint and trotted back
to the store. "Got some red and white calico?" he asked.

"Sure haven't! I'm sorry, Kid, but a fellow just came in and
bought the whole bolt. Red and white it was, too."

"What kind of a fellow?" The Kid asked suspiciously.

"A pretty salty-lookin' fellow. He was bow-legged and had a
Texas drawl."

"Why, that dirty, no-account—!" The Kid ran for his horse.

As he started out of town Reynolds flagged him down.

"Kid? What d' you make of this?" He indicated a place in the
skirt of Bantam's saddle where the stitching had been slit.
Obviously something had been hidden there. "Do you believe
that Texas man stole that money?"

"No, he was the killer, himself!"

Why Texas had headed back along the trail down which they
had come he could not guess, but that was exactly what he was
doing.

It was a gruelling chase. The paint pony liked to run, however, and although the bay was a long-legged brute they moved
up on him. Occasionally, far ahead, he glimpsed dust. Then it
dawned on him that Texas was not trying to escape. He was
simply staying enough ahead to be safe for the time being.

That could mean he planned to trap him in the hills somewhere ahead. After all, Texas had dry-gulched that other man.

When they reached the hills, the Kid turned off the trail.
This was his old stamping grounds, and he had hunted strays
all through these hills and knew their every turn and draw. He
knew Mule Creek and the Maverick Mountains like it was his
own dooryard.

Climbing the pony up the banks of the draw, the Kid skirted
a cluster of red rocks and rode down through a narrow canyon
where the ledges lay layer on layer like an enormous chocolate
cake, and emerged on a cedared hillside.

He loped the paint through the cedars, weaving a purposely
erratic path, so if observed he would not make an effective
target, then he went down into the draw, crossed the Agua
Fria, and circled back toward the trail, moving slowly with
care. He was none too soon.

Texas was loping the bay and glancing from side to side of

the trail. Almost opposite the Kid's hiding place, he reined in suddenly and swung down, headed for a bunch of rocks across the way.

The Kid stepped into the open. "It was a good idea, Texas," he said, "only I had it, too."

Startled, the man turned very slowly. "I knew you'd figure it out, Kid. I thought I'd just buy all that calico to make sure you followed me. I just don't want any witnesses left behind.

"Anyway, that girl of yours would still need a dress, and I could always say your dyin' words were that I should take it to her, and that I was to stay by an' care for her, like."

He let go of the reins of his horse. "I *would* like to know how you figured it out, though."

"It was the Henry rifle. When you rode off on the bay with the Henry in the scabbard I knew it had to be you. I found a shell from that rifle.

"Bantam was really surprised when he saw that paper. You'd slipped it into his pocket when you were standing close, then you called him a liar and killed him before he had a chance to talk. Then you went to his saddle and recovered the money."

"It was this way, Kid. I'd tailed Parsons to kill him for his money, but after I did, Bantam opened fire on me and run me off. He'd been trailing him, too. Then he went down to the body, got the money and lit out.

"Anyway," Texas added, "now you know how it was. When you came into sight, Bantam took a shot at you to warn you off until he could get out of sight.

"But I guess you got me, so it all went for nothing. I'm not sorry about Bantam, he was simply no good, but as for you—"

He would hang for what he had done, and both he and the Kid knew it, and the Kid, knowing his man, knew he would take a chance. Texas went for his gun and the Kid shot him.

Then he walked over to the bay, which showed no intention of running away, and recovered the bolt of calico, and then the money from Texas's body.

"Parsons will likely have some folks who can use this," he told himself, then rolled the body over the bank, tumbled rocks and sand over it and, gathering the reins of the bay he mounted the paint and headed for home.

When he cantered up to the gate Bonita came running, eyes sparkling with happiness. Having known other girls before, he was not sure whether it was for him or the calico, but contented himself with the conclusion it was probably a little of both.

"See?" she said. "When you just go into town and come right back there's never any trouble. It's easy to stay out of trouble if you just want to. Now this wasn't any trouble, was it?"

"No, honey, no trouble at all."

He glanced at the paint pony, who was looking at him with a skeptical eye. "You shut up!" he told the paint, and followed Bonita into the house.

The pony yawned and switched his tail at a fly.

COLONEL ALBERT PFEIFFER

The Ute and Navajo peoples had ward of ownership of the hot springs of Pagosa, in what is now Colorado. Each claimed ownership and each had some valid plans. But rather than go to war, it was decided that each tribe would choose a champion and that a battle between the two men would decide ownership of the springs.

The Navajos chose a huge warrior, a man known for his strength and fighting ability. The Utes, oddly enough, chose a white man, an adopted member of their tribe, one Colonel Albert Pfeiffer, soldier, mountainman and friend of Kit Carson.

The weapons chosen were Bowie knives, and before the assembled tribes, the two men stripped to the waist. The Navajo was a powerfully built man who towered over Pfeiffer, much the shorter of the two but nonetheless a very strong man. As they moved toward each other, Pfeiffer suddenly threw his Bowie knife with such force that it drove to the hilt in the Navajo's chest, ending the contest and deciding the issue.

HORSE HEAVEN

The high wall of the canyon threw a shadow over the entrance of the shallow cave where the two men stood, staring at the skeleton that lay on the sandy floor.

Only a few rags remained of the man's clothing, and the dried-out, twisted leather of gunbelt and boots. The front part of the head had been blown away by a bullet fired from behind. Another bullet could still be seen, lodged low down in the man's spine.

The taller and older of the two men lifted his eyes to his companion. "Are you sure it's him? There ain't much to go on, Jim."

Locklin's face was lonely. This was the last member of a once closely-knit family who lay there, the brother he had loved and admired, who had pleaded with him to come west before the War.

"I don't need anything more, Nearly. See where the left elbow was broken? I helped set it in a buffalo wallow while we fought off a bunch of Comanches.

"That gunbelt was his own work. He did it himself. He was a good man, Pike, too good a man to be trailed here and murdered after he was wounded."

"My guess would be that bullet in the spine crippled him," Nearly Pike suggested. "Why d' you suppose he came here? Was he just huntin' a place to hide? Or did he figure you'd be along?"

"He sent for me, like I told you. This is where we were to meet, so he must have had some reason why he did not want me riding down to the place without seeing him first. He'd camped here on Savory Creek before he built down in the valley, so he'd told me all about the place."

"You won't have anything to go on," Pike observed. "There's no sign left after all these years."

"There's two things. His guns are gone, so somebody packed them off, and there's the ranch. Somebody will have it, and that somebody will have some questions to answer."

He turned away. "We will come back and bury him properly when this is settled. A few more days or weeks won't matter now. From now on we are hunting two ivory-butted guns, and each will have three grooves filed in the bottom of the butt."

The trail to Toiyabe was dusty and long. Clouds hung heavy with a promise of rain, but as the hours passed it failed to develop. Wise with the wisdom of forty years west of the Missouri, Nearly Pike knew the manner of man with whom he rode. Yet he was a man who wanted nothing more than peace, and saw little in the weeks ahead.

Ten years before, George Locklin, accompanied by his much younger brother Jim, was riding through this country heading home to Texas when they saw the V where Antelope Valley points back toward a notch in the mountains. There was water and grass, with lakes and timber in the nearby hills. It was then George told his brother he had found what he wanted, and he would come back and settle on this ground and make a home for them here.

As they spoke of their plans they were sheltered in the same shallow cave on Savory Creek where his bones now lay.

Jim Locklin had stayed on in Texas, but then came the note:

Come on out, Jim, I've bought you a place called Horse Heaven, up in the mountains. I bought it in your name and filed the deed in the court house at Jacobsville. Looks like a bit of trouble here and I could use a good hand. If you don't find me around look up a man named Reed Castle.

At the time the note came Jim Locklin had been trailing north with a herd, and as they were short-handed there was no way he could leave. The mention of trouble had not alarmed him, as it had not been emphasized and he knew George could handle trouble.

They would need money to develop their property, so he took on a job ramrodding a herd from Dodge City to Canada, and then he drifted south toward Texas, pausing long enough in Deadwood to strike it rich in a small way. Finally, back in Texas, he paid off old debts and banked the rest. Only then did he start west.

"They might have buried him," Pike commented. "A man deserves that."

"I'm glad they didn't. Now I know he was murdered. He was a good man, Pike. He asked nothing from anyone and gave all he could. He could be a hard man, but this is a hard country."

"We'd best say nothing about who we are," Pike commented, as they sighted the first buildings of Toiyabe. "If we listen we might learn something."

"Good idea. You round up some grub, and I'll roust around and see what I can hear. It's been a good while, but if we can get some old timer to talkin' the rest should be easy."

Toiyabe was booming. In the bottom of its steep-walled canyon the town's few streets were jammed with freighter's outfits, the recently arrived stage, buckboards from the ranches, and horses lining the hitching rail. Aside from being the supply center for the ranches, it was also headquarters for miners and for the men who worked in the sawmill.

The Fish Creek Saloon was run by Fish Creek Burns, whose faded blue eyes had looked sadly upon a world that stretched from his boyhood in the Cumberland Gap country through Council Bluffs to the Platte and west to the Rockies and back again by way of Abilene, Dodge, El Paso, Tascosa, and Santa Fe. He was a man of many interests, few loyalties, and no illusions.

Now, suddenly, his hands stopped, utterly still, on the glass he had been polishing. A man rarely surprised, he was startled now to immobility; slowly then, after a moment, the hands began to move once more. Under the straw-colored brows, the eyes lost their momentary sharpness and assumed the faded, normal lack of lustre. Yet the mind behind them was busy.

The man who had come through the door was two inches under six feet, but broad in the chest and thick in the shoulders. He was a young man in his twenties, but compact and sharp, the lean, brown face holding the harsh lines of one much older. Fish Creek Burns never forgot a face or a loyalty.

"Rye," Locklin said mildly, "it's been a dusty ride."

"This time of year," Burns agreed, putting bottle and glass before him.

Down the bar was Chance Varrow, and behind the stranger was a poker table where one of the players was Reed Castle, of the OZ spread. Burns's eyes shifted to Locklin. "Driftin'?"

"Stayin'."

"Huntin' a job?"

"No, but maybe I'll have an outfit of my own."

Burns's tone was dry and casual as he picked up another glass. "That big man with the black mustache at the table behind you runs a lot of cattle in Antelope Valley, away back," his eyes met Locklin's, "where the valley notches the mountains."

Jim Locklin was immediately alert. What was the bartender trying to tell him? That ranch in the notch of the hills had belonged to his brother!

Burns's face was without expression. He was polishing another glass.

"Has he had the place long?"

"Three years or so. He's doing right well."

The last letter from George had been mailed just about three years ago. Jim wanted to turn and look but he did not. "Maybe he could use a hand. Does he have a name?"

"Reed Castle." Burns sighted through a glass. "He's the big man around here. A man who makes money fast makes both friends and enemies. Down the bar, the tall man in the white hat and the blue coat is Chance Varrow, and some say he could have a dozen notches on his guns if he wanted."

Varrow was taller than Locklin, with sharply-cut features, cold as a prowling fox. As Locklin looked, Varrow's eyes turned and stopped suddenly on Locklin.

"The big man in the black broadcloth suit," Burns continued, "is Creighton Burt, district attorney. A man with nerve, a man of integrity. He doesn't like Reed Castle."

Disturbed by the interest in Varrow's eyes, Jim leaned his forearms on the bar and asked Burns, "Do I look like somebody you know? Varrow acts like he's seen me somewhere."

Fish Creek kept his eyes on the glass in his hands. "Two or three years ago there was a man around here named George Locklin, and you're somewhat like him. Some said that Locklin and Varrow weren't friendly. Varrow hasn't been here long, either. Right around three years I'd say."

"Thanks. I would take it you were friendly to George Locklin?"

"He was one of the finest men I ever came across. However, I'd not speak his name about town if I were you."

"Thank you." He finished his drink. "By the way, there's a man travelin' with me. Tall old man named Nearly Pike. He may be in."

Jim Locklin managed a casual glance around the room that took in both Creighton Burt and Reed Castle. The former was large, fat, and untidy. Castle was big, and obviously prosperous. He wore a black mustache, and his face was strong-boned, a domineering face and a bold one, the face of a man who would ride rough-shod over obstacles. Jim turned and went out, letting the doors swing to behind him, turned quickly into the crowd and crossed the street. It would be a mistake to become a focus of their attention too soon.

Glancing back he saw Chance Varrow standing in the door, staring after him. Locklin went to the harness shop and, after a minute, out the side door to the alley and across to the general store where Pike was loading supplies into a couple of sacks.

Nearly Pike's Adam's apple bobbed in his scrawny throat. "Place in Hoss Heaven is lived on," he said, keeping his voice low. "Some gal moved on the place with an Injun. She's been havin' trouble with a man named Reed Castle."

Locklin was watching the street through the window. "What else?"

"Cattle range is sewed up slick and tight between four men. Reed Castle has Antelope Valley north to the mountains. John Shippey has the Monitor and Burly Ives the Smoky. Neil

Chase has the Diamond outfit. They won't let anybody drive through or in."

"Get the horses around back and load up. I'm getting some ammunition." Leaving the older man, Locklin went over to the counter.

He loved the old, familiar smell of such stores, the smell of spices, freshly ground coffee, new leather, dry goods, and the sweetish smell of gun oil.

After buying a hundred rounds of .44 ammunition, he glanced at a new shotgun, a short-barreled gun of the express-gun type carried by shotgun messengers. "Give me that scatter-gun," he said, "and a hundred rounds for it."

The storekeeper, a short, stout man, glanced up. "You must figure to fight a war with all that ammunition. And a shotgun? Never cared for 'em myself."

Locklin smiled pleasantly. "Good for quail. I like bird-meat." He loaded the shotgun. "Only empty guns that hurt folks," he commented, smiling. "I like mine loaded." He thrust the muzzle of the shotgun into the grocery sack and gathered the top of the burlap around the trigger-guard, carrying it with the stock almost invisible behind his forearm. "As for wars, I never fight unless folks push it on me. However," he paused briefly, "I plan to go into the cattle business here."

The storekeeper's head came up from the bill he was adding. "If you figure on that you'd better double your order for ammunition. This is a closed country."

"Uncle Sam doesn't say so."

"Uncle Sam doesn't run this country. The Big Four run it, and that means Reed Castle."

Jim smiled. "Ever hear," he asked gently, "of a cowman named George Locklin?"

The fat man straightened slowly, staring at him. He half turned aside, started to speak and then said nothing. Locklin went to the front door and stepped out, calling back to Pike as he did so. He stepped out right into the middle of trouble.

Confronting him was a huge back, the top of the shoulders on the level with his eyes, the vest split down the back from the strain of huge shoulders and powerful muscles. The man wore a six-shooter, and his hand gripped the butt. Beyond him

Jim could see a young Indian, straight and tall, his face expressionless. He was unarmed.

"You're a dirty, thievin' rustler!" the big man was saying. "Git! Git out of the country! We don't need your kind."

"I steal no cows."

"Don't you be callin' me no liar!" The big man's fingers grasped the gun butt tighter and he started to draw.

Locklin's left hand shot out and grasped the big man's wrist. With a startled grunt the big man began to turn, and Locklin let him turn but at the same time he shoved up and back on the gun wrist he held, pushing the elbow higher until the gun muzzle was back of the holster.

The big man struck viciously, but Locklin was too close, and the blow curled around his neck. At the same time he was shoving the big man back and keeping him off balance. The big man's back slammed against an awning-post, and Jim twisted hard on the wrist. The gun dropped from the man's fingers, and instantly Jim stepped back and drew the shotgun from the sack.

"The Indian wasn't armed," he said, "and I'll see no man murdered."

The flash of sunlight on the blue-black barrel of the shotgun had cleared the street behind the big man as if by magic.

Slowly the big man began to rub his wrist. "You'd no call to butt in, stranger. Nobody pushes Ives around."

"We've no quarrel," Locklin said, "unless you come looking for it, or unless you're one of those who murdered my brother and stole his ranch."

There was silence in the street. Somebody shifted his weight and the boardwalk creaked. "Who—? What did you say your name was?"

"My name is Locklin, Ives. Jim Locklin, brother to George Locklin who was dry-gulched and murdered up in the Monitors about three years ago."

Ives backed another step, still rubbing his wrist. He glanced around hastily as if looking for a way out or for help.

Chance Varrow stood across the street; near him was Reed Castle. "Those are hard words, friend," Varrow said. "Before you make such a statement you'd better have proof."

"I have proof of the murder. As yet I do not have the murderers."

"You are mistaken," Reed Castle said carelessly, but speaking for the onlookers more than for him. "George Locklin sold his ranch to me and left the country. Whatever you think you know is a mistake. George left here under his own power."

Jim's shotgun held steady. "Castle," he replied, his voice ringing the length of the street, "you're a liar! I have a letter from my brother telling me of the trouble he was having and asking me to come out. He had no intention of selling out, and he did have plans for developing the ranch.

"As for your ownership, I am asking right now, before the town of Toiyabe, for you to produce a bill of sale. I want to see it in the office of Creighton Burt not later than the day after tomorrow."

There was no movement; the street held its silence. Nobody realized better than Reed Castle the position he faced. Since acquiring the Antelope Valley property nothing had stopped him. His personality and strength had drawn Shippey, Chase, and Ives to him and into the combine he formed. Other cattlemen had been frozen out or driven out, and Castle was building strong and deep.

In the town itself only Creighton Burt held out against him in the open, although Castle was well aware that many lesser men both feared and hated him.

Now he had been called a liar in the open street. He had been indirectly accused of murder and theft. Nor would the story stop with the borders of this small town. It would be told and repeated in Carson, Austin, and Eureka.

"We'll make it noon, Castle. Show up with your bill of sale, and if you have one the signature had better be valid!"

Coolly, he lowered his shotgun, picked up the dropped sack, and walked across the street. Nearly Pike waited at the corner of the alley, his rifle in his hands. "Wal, son, you sure laid down your argument. Now they've got to put up or shut up."

The ride to Horse Heaven was by a devious route. Neither man knew exactly where they were going, just a general direction and some landmarks to look for. They headed northeast when leaving Toiyabe, then turned back to the southwest through Ackerman Canyon. Daylight found them camped near Antelope Peak.

From there they turned back into the hills, climbing steadily through the pines and aspen, riding warily, for they understood their situation without discussion. The easy way out, perhaps the only way, was to have Locklin killed so he could not appear at Burt's office. If he did not appear it could be shrugged off as the talk of some loud-mouthed drifter. There would be criticism, but Castle could merely say that he had been there, ready with his bill of sale, and where was this so-called Locklin fellow?

The narrow trail through the trees ended in a long basin, a grass-covered basin scattered here and there with clumps of trees and brush. On the far side, nestled against a corner of the mountain, was a cabin. A lazy trail of smoke mounted toward the sky.

"You kicked into an anthill," Pike commented. "Castle will have men ridin' the hills huntin' you."

Locklin had been thinking of that, and now they drew up in the shadow of some pines and studied the cabin and its vicinity with careful attention. A saddled horse was tied near the corral, and three other horses were loose in the corral.

As they watched, two people came into sight, a girl from the cabin and an Indian from the rocks near the cliff. "That's the Injun you spoke for, Jim. I'd know that odd limp anywhere."

They had no sooner broken from cover than they were seen. The girl started toward the cabin, but something said by the Indian stopped her, and she turned back.

What he had expected he was not sure, but certainly not what he found. She was a tall, beautifully shaped girl with dark skin, from which her gray eyes were both startling and lovely. She studied him carefully as he drew near, but she was by no means frightened. She had poise and manner, and seemed perfectly sure of herself. The Indian was wearing a gun now.

"Howdy, ma'am," Jim said. "I'm Locklin. I own this place."

"I know who you are. As to owning this place, that's a matter for discussion. Get down and come in, will you? Patch told me what you did for him."

Inside she busied herself putting food on the table and

getting coffee started. "I'm Army Locklin. Army being short for Armorel, the Locklin because I was married to your brother."

"You were *what?*"

"We were married the day he disappeared. He got word of trouble at the ranch just after reaching town. He left me in town and rushed back to the place and right into an ambush. He was shot down, got away into the brush, and that was the last he was seen."

"I don't know what to say. George said nothing of you in his letters."

She smiled bitterly. "He did not know me then. I came to Toiyabe to marry Reed Castle, but we did not see eye to eye on several subjects, and I refused to go through with it.

"Reed became angry and threatened me, then he tried to get the people at the hotel to turn me out. George had had trouble with Reed, so when he heard of it he came to me and offered his assistance."

Her eyes turned to Jim. "I was alone in the world, and it had taken the last of my money to come here from San Francisco. I told George I did not love him, but if he really wanted me I'd try to become a good wife. We were married, but I never had a chance to be anything to him.

"Now," she added, "you know why I have no use for Castle, and why he wants me out of the country."

"How'd you meet him in the first place?"

"My father died, and he did not leave me very much. I had friends back east who knew Reed Castle, and they told him about me and sent him a picture. He proposed by mail. It all seemed very romantic, a handsome western rancher and all that."

"Why did you suggest I might not own this place?"

"You own half of it. I own the other half. I filed a claim on the land that lies alongside of your ranch.

"You see, George gave me money when we were married. He did not have all that much, but he did not want me to feel bound, and if I was unhappy I could leave whenever I wished.

"After George disappeared Reed came forward with a bill of sale and claimed the ranch. He said George had changed his mind about being married to me, had sold the ranch and skipped out. I did not believe a word of it, but I could prove nothing. Everybody was feeling very sorry for me, but after all, I had not known George but a few days, and he *might* have decided marriage was not for him. I could prove nothing."

"But you stayed on?"

"There was nowhere to go. George might reappear. And then, George had told me you were coming." She paused. "Did—did George ever mention a silver strike? Not far from here?"

"Silver?" He frowned, trying to think back. There had been a number of letters, early on. "No, I don't think so."

Then he indicated the bunkhouse where the Indian had gone. "What about Patch? Where does he fit in?"

"I don't know. I honestly don't. He rode in here one day on a flea-bitten roan pony, and wanted to work for me. I did need help, but had so little money. He told me he wanted to work for me and I could pay him when I wished. Since then he has worked hard, has been loyal, too, only when Reed Castle is around he always gets out of sight. I think he may be afraid of him."

"Why do you call him Patch? Is he an Apache?"

"He is, but he would give me no name, so I began calling him that."

There was no accounting for Indians. They had their own ideas, and followed them. Few Apaches could be found this far north and west, for they loved their southwestern desert country, but there were wanderers from all tribes.

Reed Castle was no fool. Crooked he might be, but he was also intelligent and shrewd, and the two were rarely the same thing. He would know that any bill of sale he might have would be an obvious forgery, so he must have other irons in the fire. Of course, he knew George Locklin was dead, and he had had nothing to worry about until now.

Jim Locklin wanted more than simply to recover the ranch. He wanted to face the man who had killed George. At this date the proof would be hard to come by, but the more he thought about it the more he wondered. George had always been a thorough man who left little to chance, and he had lived long enough to reach the cave on Savory Creek. As he certainly had not lived with that hole in his head, he must have received the spinal wound first, but had somehow kept going until he reached the cave.

He had undoubtedly been helpless when he was killed, but had he been helpless when he arrived? How much time had he before his lower limbs became paralyzed?

With a growing feeling of excitement, Jim Locklin got up and went to the bunkhouse. His brother had always been one to communicate. He always left messages behind him. One never had to guess with George. He always had a plan. There had been a hollow in the rocks on the old L Bar, and there had been a rock under a tree on the way to Toiyabe where they exchanged messages.

So why not now, of all times? If he had struggled to reach that cave with almost his last strength, it must have been done with purpose.

Excited though he was, he finally dropped off, and, tired from travel, he slept deeply.

He awakened to daybreak and angry voices. Hurriedly, he threw on some clothing and, grabbing his rifle, went to the door. His breath caught sharply as he saw Ives and several of his riders. Patch was nowhere in sight, but one of Ives's men had a rifle on Pike and Army.

Resting his rifle against the door jam he called out, "Looking for me, Burly? I'm right here!"

Ives turned sharply in his saddle, but only the rifle indicated Locklin's presence. And the rifle was aimed at him.

The bunkhouse walls were too solid to shoot through, and Ives was no longer in command of the situation. If shooting started it was quite obvious who would get shot first.

A rattle of horses' hoofs distracted his attention, and when Locklin followed Burly's gaze he saw a half-dozen riders led by a square-built, oldish man with a white mustache. "What's goin' on here, Burly? You're not goin' to make trouble for that girl while I'm around!"

"Keep out of this, John! I came here to settle things with this here Locklin."

Jim put down the rifle and reached to the empty upper bunk for the shotgun he had left there. "If you want to settle things with me, why bring your whole outfit?" He stepped out into the yard. "Or do you think you need all that help to handle one man?"

"Put down that shotgun and I'll break you in half!"

Locklin handed the shotgun to Pike. "Get down off that horse and we'll see." He glanced at the white-haired man. "I take it you are John Shippey? Will you see that I get fair play?"

"Your durned tootin' I will!" He waved a hand. "Everybody stand back and let them have at it. Anybody who tries to interfere will settle with me."

Burly unbuckled his gun belts with great good humor and hung them on the saddle horn. Having little stomach for gunfights, he relished a chance to use his fists. That he had never been whipped helped him to anticipate the fight.

"He'll make two of you, son!" Pike protested. "Look at the size of him!"

Locklin ignored him. He was intent upon Ives now, and thinking only of him. He moved in swiftly. He circled warily. It was obvious from Burly's manner that he was no stranger to fighting, yet when the big man moved his first tentative blow was short. Locklin feinted a move, side-stepped quickly and smashed Ives in the mouth. The blow landed solidly, and blood splashed from badly cut lips. Locklin started to draw away and it was all that saved him. A hard right on the ear knocked him staggering, and Burly rushed, his greater height, weight, and reach driving Locklin back, off balance. Jim landed a couple of ineffective blows to the body.

Jim caught a hard blow and went down. Ives, carried forward by the impetus of his rush, tried a hasty kick and missed. Locklin came up fast, his head still buzzing from the blow he'd caught, and he went under a left and smashed both hands to the body. Neither man knew more of fighting than what they had learned by applying it, but both were skilled in the rough-and-tumble style of the frontier which they had been using since boyhood.

Locklin bored in, went under a swing with a right to the body, then an overhand left that split Ives's ear and staggered him. Instantly, Locklin was on him, his blows ripping and slashing at the bigger man.

Ives struggled to get set, striking back with heavy, ponderous blows. Suddenly, Locklin ceased to punch and, diving low, grabbed Ives around the knees and upended him.

Ives hit the dirt with a thud, but he rolled over like a cat and came to his feet. Jim was set for him, and caught him with a hard right that cracked like a ball bat. Then Jim rushed in close and began to batter at Ives's body.

Ives was badly cut, and one of his eyes almost closed, yet Locklin was weary simply from punching and holding the larger man off.

He put his head on the bigger man's chest and punched at his body with both hands. Ives, an old river-boat fighter, stabbed at his eyes with a stiff thumb, but Locklin dropped his head to Ives's chest again and suddenly smashed upward with his head, butting him on the chin. Ives staggered, and Locklin swung with both fists for his chin, left and right.

Ives went down hard. He got up slowly, warily. Jim Locklin had backed off, gasping for breath. He started to circle, his foot slipped, and Ives grabbed him in a bear hug, forcing him back. Excruciating pain stabbed him, and Jim fought desperately to free himself, knowing the larger man was strong enough to break his back.

Suddenly, Jim deliberately threw himself backward. He hit the ground hard, but it broke Ives's hold, and Jim got to his feet. Ives dove at him to bring him down again, and Locklin met the dive by jerking up his knee into Ives's face.

The big man went to hands and knees, his features a blur of blood. Locklin waited, gasping. Ives started to rise, and Locklin moved in. A left and right, then a terrific right uppercut that snapped the big man's head back. He went down to his knees, then toppled over on the grass.

Jim staggered back, his jaw hanging as he gasped for breath, waiting for Ives to rise.

"Let him go, Locklin," John Shippey said. "He's whipped." Then he added, "I never thought I'd see the day!"

Seated in the kitchen, Army bathed Locklin's face, tenderly wiping the blood from his features. "You've got some bad cuts," she protested.

"They'll heal," he said. "They always did before."

Pike was explaining the situation to Shippey. He had gotten
George Locklin's letters from a saddlebag, and showed them to
the rancher. "Those were writ by no man who thought of
sellin'!" Pike insisted.

Locklin pushed Army's hands gently aside. He got to his
feet, staggering a little. His big hands were swollen and battered. "Shippey, I won't get into town in time. It would be a
favor if you'd ride in and hold Burt an' Castle until I get there.
Nearly Pike will ride with you."

"Where you goin'?" Pike demanded.

"I've had a thought, and if I'm right we'll have our killer."

John Shippey nodded his head. "I'll do my best." He turned
suddenly to Pike. "Where'd you get a name like that?"

"Wal, it was like this here, Mr. Shippey. My folks was
named Pike. We headed west from Kentucky for Missouri.
Bein' named Pike, we figured to live in Pike County, and I was
to be born there. Well, we didn't make it. We had to stop
some miles short, so they named me for it. Nearly Pike."

Army was looking at Locklin, an odd light in her eyes, a look
of something close to fear. Women, Jim reflected, would never
understand a man's fighting.

Ives got slowly to his feet, staggered a little, then stood
erect. His face was a mask of blood and dirt. He leaned against
his horse for a moment, then hoisted himself into the saddle.
He said nothing until he had gathered the reins. "You're a hard
man, Locklin," he said grudgingly, "I reckon I bit off more'n I
could chaw."

Locklin watched him go, then turned to his horse, which
Pike had saddled and ready. Army came to him. "Don't go,
Jim! I'm afraid! And you're in no shape to go!"

He tried to smile, but his face was too swollen. He leaned
over and put a hand on her shoulder. "You ride to town with
them. Stay close to Pike. This is something I must do."

Jim Locklin rode toward Antelope Valley, then took a dim
trail up to the bench. He rode through the pines, his face
throbbing with every hoof-beat, his ribs aching from the bruises.
His head ached and the sun was hot. At Butler Creek he
dropped on his face and drank deep of the clear, cold mountain
water. Then he bathed his face with it.

Rising, he glimpsed the tracks of two people across the narrow stream. Crossing on scattered rocks in the stream-bed he studied the tracks with care. Some were fresh, yet others were older. Obviously, whoever they were, they had met here several times. Some cowhand and his girl, no doubt.

He went back across the stream to his horse but as he started to mount the combination of sun and the fighting proved too much. He backed up and sat down on the grass. Then he dragged himself back into the shade and slept.

He awakened suddenly. A glance at the sun told him he had slept for all of an hour, yet despite the fact that his head still throbbed, he felt better. Later, he cut the tracks of one rider, heading toward Horse Heaven. The tracks were several days old.

He turned down into the canyon of the Savory, and almost at once was enclosed by towering walls, and the sound of the stream rose in volume. Then the canyon widened, and before him was a sandy shelf strewn with the gray bones of ancient trees. Beyond it, the cave.

Swinging down, he leaned against the saddle to still the momentary dizziness that beset him. Then he walked up to the cave.

He stopped then, quite abruptly, his mouth dry but his brain sharply alert. He was looking into the peculiar white-gray eyes of Chance Varrow!

There was a taunting triumph in Varrow's eyes. "Took you long enough to get here. Long enough so I could beat you to it. Now you can die the way your brother died. Funny, you blaming Reed Castle. He had the idea, all right, but we beat him to it."

"You killed George?" Even as he spoke he was thinking less of what he was saying and more of his own swollen, battered hands and the gun-slick deftness of the man he faced.

"Sure! At least I finished him off. He was already down and crippled. Reed wanted that ranch, all right, and was trying to work out some way of gettin' it. Well, we wasted no time.

"He could have the ranch, because we knew of that silver strike he'd made, near Bald Mountain. We gambled on that, and now we've won."

"Are you sure?"

"Why not? Nobody knows I'm in this but Reed Castle, and he wouldn't talk. If he did nobody would believe him. Your coming upset things but that's ended now."

Locklin's mind was working swiftly. Who did he mean by "we"? How had Varrow known he would be coming to the cave?

Ives? Probably.

But why, in all this time, had they not taken possession of the silver strike, sold it, and skipped? The reason was obvious—they didn't know where it was!

"You're not killing me, Varrow. It's not in the cards, no more than your friend Ives could whip me. It's you who will die here in this cave, Varrow, right here on this sand.

"You've wasted your time and your killing. You've never laid hands on an ounce of that silver because you don't know where it is.

"I know where it is," he lied, "and if I die you will never get it. Why? Because nobody else knows, nobody at all!"

"I'm going to kill you, all right," Varrow's face was tight and cruel. "I'll gamble on finding the silver."

Locklin swayed on his feet, suddenly weak. "A thousand have looked for it, and nobody found it until George, and he had a clue. He knew something nobody else knew. The same thing he passed on to me."

At the first sign of faintness Chance Varrow's hand dropped to his gun. Suddenly Locklin's knees buckled and he went to the sand. Then he sagged back on his heels. "Sorry, Varrow, I'm in pret—ty bad—" he lifted a trembling hand to his brow, yet even as the hand seemed to touch his face, it darted like a striking snake, spraying sand in Varrow's face!

The gunman sprang back, one hand clawing at his eyes, the other reaching for his gun. His gun came clear, but the moment's respite was all Locklin needed. He got his clumsy fingers on his own gun, swung it up, steadied it with the other hand, and fired!

Varrow's gun roared, but, blinded by the sand, he missed.

Locklin's bullet, at point-blank range, caught Varrow in the diaphragm, striking up and in. Varrow tried to swing his gun, but Locklin fired a second time, then a third.

Chance Varrow crumpled into the sand, his fingers relaxing their grip on the gun.

The gunshots echoed in the canyon and there was an acrid smell of gunpowder mingled with dusty dampness. Then the echoes died, and there was only the soft chuckling of water over stones.

Dusk was blending the shadows in the streets of Toiyabe when Jim Locklin cantered down the street and drew up at the hotel door. Pike rushed out and grabbed his stirrup leather. "You all right, boy? I been out of my skull with worry."

"Where are they, Pike?"

"Inside. What took you so long?"

"A bit of trouble." All eyes turned to him as he entered. Castle's looked pale, angry, and uneasy; those of Creighton Burt, John Shippey, and Fish Creek Burns indicated only sharp interest. Armorel Locklin stared at him, her eyes showing her anxiety. Patch, looking surly, sat behind her.

Locklin leaned his hands on the table. "Castle, I had you wrong. You are a thief, but you are not a murderer."

"I bought that ranch!" Castle protested. "Here's my bill of sale!"

"An obvious forgery. The trouble was, you had never actually seen my brother's signature. You didn't worry because nobody else had, either. I have several letters signed by him, and I also have his will. The will was written as he was dying, with the knowledge that he was dying, and he leaves the ranch and all property to me, including the mine on Bald Mountain."

"What about this young woman? She was his wife."

"That's just it," Jim's eyes turned to Army. "She never was his wife."

"I married them," Burt said quietly, "right in my own office."

"The marriage wasn't valid, because she was still married to Chance Varrow."

"What? Are you sure?"

"I am sure. The two of them were teamed up, trimming suckers out in Frisco, and when Reed came to town flashing money around and talking big about his ranch and mining interests, they latched onto him.

"Army came over here to marry him, then found out he had

lied, and backed out. Chance had come along to enforce her claim, and he got wind of George's silver strike.

"They let Reed Castle keep the ranch to quiet him down." Locklin drew a deep breath. He was tired, very tired. He wanted this over, he wanted to be away from here. "She has takin' ways, this girl does, and I nigh fell for her myself. George left me a note telling me all about it.

"She found him alone and lonesome, buttered him up some, let him think he was saving her from Castle, and then, after they left town, she shot him in the back.

"That back shot puzzled me, for George was touchy about anybody coming up behind him. I couldn't see a man getting such a chance, but a woman might. As she shot him, Chance came out of the woods to finish him, but George got away.

"Varrow had to wait until daylight to pick up the trail, and by that time George had left his horse and crawled into the cave. His legs were paralyzed, but he wrote the details, then stuffed his notes, his will, what else he had, into a tin box he kept there.

"On that sandstone he scratched the old L Bar brand that would mean nothing to anybody but us."

"Where's Varrow, then?" Shippey demanded. "Let's get the sheriff and round him up."

Army's eyes were on Jim, wide and empty. She knew, and he could see that she knew.

"He was waiting for me at the cave. I left him there."

Jim dropped the notes and the will on the table before Burt. "There it is. There was enough to hang Varrow, and enough to send Castle away for a good long stretch."

Burt glanced at Patch. "Where does he fit in?"

"She my half-sister," Patch said sullenly. "She no good. Some white man bad, some Indian bad. She no good."

Locklin looked over at Patch, liking what he saw. "You want a job? A permanent job?"

"Uh-huh. I work good."

Army's eyes were sullen with hatred. Having them know she was a 'breed bothered her more than being accused of murder. Jim looked at her, marveling. When would people realize it wasn't race that mattered, but quality and integrity?

"How'd you work it out?" Burt wondered.

"The first thing was the back shot; then George's guns were gone. Later, I saw them hanging on a nail in her cabin. George's holsters and belt with his name carved into them were left; only his guns were taken.

"George took those guns off for nobody, and the holsters in the cabin weren't his. That started me on the right track.

"Then I found tracks where she and Varrow had been meeting over on Butler Creek. My head was aching so bad I could scarcely think; then it dawned on me where I'd seen her tracks before. Varrow's I did not know.

"My brother had seen her talking to Varrow one time, but did not want to believe there was anything between them."

Locklin got to his feet. "That winds it up." He looked over at Castle. "I'm moving onto the Antelope Valley place tomorrow. All your personal effects will be sent to town."

The door opened behind them, and a short, heavy man stepped into the door. "I'm Jacob Carver, of Ellsworth, Kansas. I'm holding six hundred head of cattle outside of town, but I hear you folks got this country closed up. Is that right?"

Shippey started to speak but Locklin interrupted. "No, of course not. There's some unused range up in Grass Valley, northwest of here. As long as a man is honest and a good neighbor we've room for him. Glad to have you."

As Carver left Locklin glanced at Shippey. "He's a good man. I knew his brand back in Kansas. This country can use his kind."

Locklin left followed by Pike. Fish Creek Burns glanced after him, then said, glancing from Shippey to Burt. "Things are clearin' up around here, and she looks like fair weather ahead."

He stood up. "Looks like we've got a new pair of pants in the saddle. It surely does!"

CLAY ALLISON

Almost any old-timer in West Texas or New Mexico had a Clay Allison story. He was a cattleman and a former Confederate soldier, reported to have ridden with Nathan Bedford Forrest, one of the greatest. Born in Tennessee in 1840, he had come West after the War, had ridden up the Goodnight-Loving Trail with Charles Goodnight (who invented the chuck wagon) and had begun ranching with his brother, John.

A handsome man but of uncertain temper, he had settled several disputes with gunfire, and later rumor was to credit him with at least 30 killings. This figure is no doubt exaggerated as most such figures were, yet on one occasion the six gun was not the weapon selected.

During a bitter dispute with a neighboring rancher, the other man protested, "Don't go for your gun, Clay! The gun is not my weapon!"

"Then what is?" Clay asked.

"The Bowie knife."

"All right, we will dig a grave, six feet deep, six feet long. You stand at one end with your knife and I will stand at the other end with mine. The winner fills it in."

Sometime later, with a bad wound in his thigh, and with several minor cuts and abrasions, Clay filled it in.

SQUATTERS ON THE
LONETREE

Tanner was fastening the tailgate when Wiley Dunn saw him and started across the street. Algosa held its collective breath, for this was the first meeting between the owner of Hat and the nester who had squatted on Lonetree.

For fifteen years Wiley Dunn and his hard-bitten Hat riders had ruled unchallenged over two hundred thousand acres of range, growing in wealth and power. Occasionally, ill-advised nesters had moved on Hat range, but the only nesters still there were buried. The others had departed hurriedly for parts as far away as possible. Tanner was the exception. He had squatted on a small, rugged corner with a lovely green meadow where there was plenty of both timber and water.

Dunn was a square, powerful man who walked with quick, knee-jerking strides. That Tanner defied his power nettled him. He could see no sense in the man starting a fight he had no chance of winning.

Tanner straightened as Dunn approached, and Dunn was startled to find his eyes piercingly black, although the nester's hair was a faded rust color. Tanner had a lean body, slightly stooped.

"Howdy, Dunn. Been aimin' to see you. Some of your critters been watering down around Sandy Point and getting caught in quicksand. You ought to have your hands throw up a fence."

79

"Thanks." Dunn was brusque. "Tanner, you have forty-eight hours to get off my range."

Tanner took a slow drag on his cigarette. "Now, Mr. Dunn, you know better than to tell me that. If I was fixin' to leave at all I'd have been long gone. That place appeals to me, so we're just a-stayin' on."

"Don't be a fool!" Dunn said impatiently. "You haven't a chance! My cattle have been grazing that range for years, and we're not about to give it up to some two-by-twice nester who comes driftin' into the country. I've got forty tough cowhands, and if you persist, I'll—"

"You'll get some of them hurt. Now look here, Mr. Dunn. You've got a sight of range out there, and it's all government land. I'm not takin' much of it, so you just leave me alone."

"Be reasonable!" Dunn was not anxious to fight. He had done his share of fighting. "You can't make a living on that piece of ground."

"I aim to raise some shoats," Tanner said, squinting against the sun. "Put me in a few acres of corn." He indicated the sacks in the wagon. "Got my seed already."

"Hogs? This is beef country!"

"So I figure to raise hogs. Folks like a mite of side meat, time to time."

"You get off that land in forty-eight hours." Dunn was growing impatient. He was used to issuing ultimatums that were instantly obeyed, not to discussing them. He was also aware the whole town was watching.

"Look, Mr. Dunn, my folks and I like that little place. We can be right neighborly, but we can also be a mite mean, if pressed.

"We've got little to lose. You've got plenty. I don't want a fight, but if you start it I won't set and wait. I'll come after you, Mr. Dunn. I'll bring the fight to you."

Enraged, Dunn turned away, yet it was disappointment as much as anger. He had hoped there would be no fight, but if this man stayed, others would move in. None of them would make it. And when they started to go hungry they would start killing his cattle. He had seen it happen before. Moreover, the man baffled him. Tanner should have been frightened or worried. He was neither.

"Boss," Ollie Herndon suggested, "let me take him? He's askin' for it."

"No, no!" Dunn protested. "I won't have a man killed with his wife and children looking on."

"That's his wife's brother," Turner said, "they've only been married a couple of years."

"You let me have him," Herndon said. "He's too durned sure of hisself."

"Funny thing," Turner commented, "this is the third time I've seen that wagon in town, but I've yet to see tracks comin' from his place."

"What's that mean?" Dunn demanded.

"You figure it out, Boss. I surely can't."

Despite his determination to rid himself of the nester, Dunn knew the man would be a hard nut to crack, and it would be apt to create quite a stir if there was a killing. And there could be.

Tanner had built his house of stone right against the face of a limestone cliff in the small valley of the Lonetree, a place approachable only from the front. Tanner was reputed to be a dead shot. Yet there was a way—catch him in an open field.

Hat made its try the following day.

Eight riders slipped close under protection of the willows, then charged. Tanner was in plain sight in the open pasture, nothing near him for shelter but a few scattered rock piles, bushes, and trees.

"Got him!" Ollie yelled triumphantly. "Now we'll show him!"

They rushed first to cut him off from the house, then swept down upon him. Only he was no longer there.

Tanner had vanished like a puff of smoke, and then a rifle boomed. A horse went down, spilling his rider; another boom, and the hat was knocked from Ollie's head. As the riders swirled past where they had seen Tanner they found nothing, absolutely nothing! It was unbelievable.

The angry riders circled. "Shots came from those rocks," one maintained.

"No, it was from that clump of brush."

A rifle boomed from the house, and one of the horses started pitching wickedly. When the horse ceased bucking, a scattering of shots caused them to scatter in flight. Hastily, they hunted cover.

"It ain't possible!" Ollie protested. "We all seen him! Right out there in plain sight!"

At daybreak the following morning, irritated by the report of the previous day's events, Wiley Dunn was up pacing the floor. He walked out on the wide veranda, and something caught his attention.

Three large watermelons lay on the edge of the porch, beside them a sack of roasting ears. Pinned to the sack was a note:

Figured these would go well with beef. Better keep your outfit to home. They git kind of carried away with theirselves.

Wiley Dunn swore bitterly, glaring at the melons. Sobering a little, he decided they did look mighty tasty.

Ollie Herndon's report worried him. Dropped from sight, Ollie said. Obviously the mountain man had been concealed in the brush, but why hadn't they found him? Ollie was no pilgrim. He should have been able to smoke him out.

Three days went by before they attacked again. Ollie led this one, too, and he had seven men. They rode to within a few hundred yards, then concealed their horses and approached on foot. They did not talk, and they had waited until it was good and dark before they began their approach. They could see the lights in the cabin, and they started across the field through the grass, walking carefully. They were halfway across when Ollie suddenly tripped, staggered, and fell. Instantly a gun boomed.

Flat on their faces in the grass, they lay cursing. That shot had been close, and it sounded like a shotgun.

Ollie ran his fingers through the grass. "Wire!" he said with disgust. "A durned trip-wire!" He glanced up. The lights were gone.

Ollie was furious. To be tricked by a damned nester! He got to his feet and the others arose with him. Red moved closer to

Ollie. "No use goin' up there now. That ol' catamount's ready for us."

It was a fact understood by all. There was literally nothing else they could do. The stone house was situated in such a position that one had to cross the meadows to approach it, and the corrals, stock, and hay were all in a box canyon entered from beside the house. To get nearer without being heard was no longer possible, and shooting at the stone house would simply be a waste, as well as dangerous. It was a thousand to one against their scoring a hit, and their gun-flashes would reveal their positions, making them good targets in the open meadow.

Disgusted, they trooped, grumbling, back to their horses and rode back to the ranch.

Wiley Dunn was irritated. The continued resistance of Tanner was not only annoying and disconcerting, but was winning friends for Tanner. Even his own lawyer made a sly comment on it, but to Dunn it was not amusing. He had hoped that Tanner could be pushed off without any real bloodshed, but it appeared that the only way to be rid of him was to kill him. Ten years ago he would not have hesitated, but the times had changed, and people were looking askance at big outfits running rough-shod over people.

He was tempted to turn Ollie Herndon loose, but hesitated. There should be some other way. If he could only catch Tanner on the road and destroy his place while he was gone.

Somehow the story had gotten around that Dunn's hands had failed in an attack on the Lonetree nester and he had repaid them with watermelons. The next time Dunn appeared in town Ed Wallis asked, "How were the melons, Wiley? Didn't upset your stomach, did they?"

Dunn's smile faded. "That nester's askin' for it. He's been warned to get off my place!"

"It ain't like it was, Wiley. Why don't you let him be? A man like that might prove to be a good neighbor. He seems a decent sort."

"Look, Ed, if I allowed Tanner to stay on that place my range would be over-run by squatters. Besides, in a bad year I'd need that water."

Wallis shrugged. "It's none of my affair, although folks are saying that with two hundred thousand acres you should let a man have enough to live on. As for water, you'd have plenty of water, and grass, too, if you didn't over-graze. You've got more cattle on that grass than it can carry."

"You tellin' me my business? I've been in the cow business twenty-five years, and no small potatoes storekeeper is going to tell me how to do it."

Ed Wallis turned abruptly. "Sorry I spoke to you, Dunn. It is none of my business. You handle your own affairs." He returned to his store.

Wiley Dunn stared after him, angry at Wallis but even more angry at himself. What was he getting mad at Ed for? They had been friends for fifteen years. But that talk about carrying too much stock was stupid, although, in a year like this when he was going to be in a tight for feed, it might make sense. It was that damned nester's fault, he decided. If Tanner hadn't moved onto that range he would have been all right.

He started along the street to the post office, and was just turning in at the door when Tanner and his wife came out.

Tanner was no more than thirty at best, his wife a good ten years younger, a quietly pretty girl whose eyes widened when she saw him. That she was frightened angered Dunn even more. What kind of a person was he supposed to be, that a young woman should be afraid of him? What had Tanner been telling her?

"Tanner," he said abruptly, "have you moved yet?"

Tanner smiled. "Why, howdy, Mr. Dunn! No, we haven't moved and we don't plan to. That's government land, Mr. Tanner, and you've no rightful claim to it. On the other hand, I've filed on it for a homestead. All we want is to make a livin', so leave us alone, Mr. Dunn."

People were listening, and Wiley Dunn was aware of it. There was such a thing as prestige, and by simply telling the Tanners they might stay on undisturbed he could have established a reputation of another kind; on the other hand, he had lived so long with the psychology of the feudal baron it was not in him to change quickly. This Tanner had to be put in his place.

"Now you see here, Tanner. I am not going to fool around any longer. You're on my water and I want you off. You get off now, or you'll answer to me. I'll send my men around to take care of you."

"What's the matter, Mr. Dunn?" Tanner's voice was suddenly soft, but something in it brought Wiley Dunn up short. "Can't you fight your own battles? Have you been hidin' behind Ollie Herndon so long you don't remember what it means to get a bloody nose?"

Wiley Dunn stared at Tanner. Not for years had anyone dared challenge him. Not for years had he had a fight of any kind. He was a burly, husky man who had won many a rough-and-tumble fight in years gone by, but there was something about Tanner that warned Dunn he would be hard to handle. Yet Dunn had had the reputation of being a fighter, and he had won it the hard way.

"I don't mix in dirty brawls, Tanner. It won't be a matter of fists if I come after you."

Tanner was no longer smiling. "Mr. Dunn, I have never hunted trouble with any man, although here and there trouble has come to me. I've not hunted trouble with you, but your boys have attacked my home twice.

"Now, Mr. Dunn, I've always hoped I'd never have to kill another man, but if it is guns you want it is guns you can have. Right now, right here at this minute, if you want it that way. I'm carrying a gun, Mr. Dunn. Are you?"

Wiley Dunn felt butterflies in his stomach. Maybe he was getting old. "No," he said honestly, "I am not carrying a gun, but—"

Sheriff Collins had been watching and now he stepped in. "All right, break it up! There will be no talk of guns while I'm sheriff of this county." Collins looked at Tanner, his expression harsh. The sheriff was a cattleman himself. "Do you hear that, Tanner?"

"I hear it," Tanner replied calmly, "but while you're at it, you tell Dunn to keep his men away from my place. They've attacked me twice, with guns."

"I know nothing about that," Collins replied stiffly. "If you want to file a complaint, I will act upon it."

"I've always fought my own battles, Sheriff, but I would like to call your attention to something. You were standing here listening when he threatened me and ordered me off land on which I have legally filed. If there is a court case I'll certainly have you called as a witness."

He turned to his wife. "Sorry, honey, I didn't mean to keep you waitin'."

Slowly the crowd dispersed. Only Collins and Dunn remained.

For a few moments nothing was said, then Dunn spoke. "I wish the damned fool would move off that place! I don't want trouble, Jim, but I need that water."

"You've got water elsewhere. You've a lot of land, Wiley. Maybe you should pull in your horns."

"And let him whip me?"

"Can't you see, Wiley? Tanner ain't tryin' to whip you. He wants to stay. Why don't you slap him on the back and tell him if he gives you a piece of side meat from time to time he can stay."

There was good sense in what Collins advised, and Collins was a good man. "But I can't let him get away with this, Jim. He called me to my face. Nobody has done that since the Powell boys."

Wiley Dunn had killed the Powell boys, all three of them. He had been fourteen years younger then, but he was still, he told himself, a tough man.

"You're asking for it, Wiley, but let me give you a word of advice from a friend. Don't get the idea that Tanner is easy. He ain't."

On his way back to the ranch, Wiley Dunn mulled that over, and he had to admit his impression was the same. There was something in Tanner's manner that warned Dunn that the man was no pilgrim. And what was that Tanner had said? That he did not want to kill *another* man?

Suddenly he remembered what Rowdy or somebody had said about there being no tracks leaving Tanner's place. What could that mean?

His curiosity aroused, Dunn turned the bay off the trail to the ranch and cut across the hill to the county road. It took him only a few minutes to find the tracks of Tanner's returning buckboard, his saddle horse tied behind. For three miles he followed the tracks and then, suddenly, they were gone.

Puzzled, he reined the bay around and rode back. Crushed grass told him where Tanner had turned off, and he followed the tracks over a low hill and alongside a dry wash. He was now not more than five miles from Tanner's cabin, but separated from it by the bulk of Wildhorse Mesa, a huge block of basaltic rock some four hundred feet high by eight miles long, and at least two miles wide. If this was the route Tanner took to his home, it was far out of the way.

Turning back, Dunn reached the trail and started for the ranch. Frowning, he considered what he had learned. It seemed stupid for a man to go so far out of his way to avoid trouble on the trail, yet going over the mesa was an impossibility. It was true, he had never skirted the mesa on the north, but he had been within a quarter of a mile many times on the south side, and the steep talus slides ended in an abrupt cliff, at least a hundred feet of sheer rock.

Maybe he was being a damned fool. After all, Lonetree lay far from the home ranch and they had rarely watered there, holding it rather for emergencies than otherwise. He could let it go and never miss it. Irritably, he shook off the thought. The land was his, and he was going to keep it.

Had he persisted in trailing Tanner he would have had a further surprise. In such broken, rugged country, even a man who has lived and ridden there for years sometimes misses things. Had he been skirting the mesa on foot, something no cowhand would dream of doing, he would have discovered it was not, as it seemed, a continuous wall.

A few days after Tanner had completed the building of the stone house in Lonetree Canyon, he had taken his rifle and ridden out to hunt for a deer. Picketing his horse on a patch of grass, he had taken his rifle and walked up a tiny creek toward its beginning at the mesa's base.

He drank from the spring, then straightened up and turned west. He was wiping his mouth with the back of his hand when he realized he was looking at a break in the wall of the mesa. Moreover, there was a dim game trail leading from the spring back into the notch.

The trail entering the opening went in parallel with the mesa's wall, which was fractured, leaving one point of rock extended along the face of the mesa so that from a short distance away it appeared to be one unbroken wall.

Following the dim trail through talus and broken rock, and pushing through brush, he found that it turned sharply south, and he was standing in a gap where the mesa was actually separated into two. Lying before him was a meadow at least a hundred yards wide. Following it, he discovered that at one place it became almost a half-mile wide, then narrowed again as it neared the north side. At the lowest point there was a small lake, almost an acre in extent. The opening on the far side emerged in a thick stand of aspen, and in the distance he could see the smoke from Algosa. Not only had he discovered a private trail out of his ranch, but added grazing and a much shorter route to town.

From the Bar 7, a ranch several miles to the west, he bought twenty young heifers, and turned them into the grassy basin. Then he prepared a pole gate and fence at the far end, and another at his own end of the opening.

Each time he used the route through the mesa he took care to cover his tracks, wiping them out near a shelf of rock so the tracks seemed to vanish on the rock itself. Over the way into the aspen he placed a dead tree, still attached to its base by a few shreds of wood. This he could swing back and forth, making the route seem impassable to a buckboard.

When Morgan Tanner returned to the stone house, he helped Ann from the buckboard. For a moment she stood close to him. "Will they ever leave us alone, Morgan?"

"I believe they will. There will be trouble first, I think. Ollie Herndon is hunting trouble, with or without orders from Dunn. We've got to be careful."

During subsequent days he explored the rift in the mesa, finding several ice caves, and in one of them a stone hammer. He prowled the canyon, often alone, but sometimes with either Johnny Ryan or Ann. He did a lot of thinking about what he had discovered.

Algosa was no longer just a cowtown. Mines were being opened in the back country; although not very rich they had large ore bodies and gave evidence they might last, turning Algosa into a market town.

Morgan Tanner had come from mountain country where cattle were more valued for milk, butter, and cheese than for beef, but so far as he was aware the only milk cow in Algosa was owned by the postmaster.

What Dunn might be planning he could not guess, but the raids ceased. Tanner rarely went to town, and the place was never empty. When he did go into town he met people, and he asked a few questions, listened a lot.

Johnny Ryan, his wife's brother, was a hardworking youngster of thirteen. With Johnny helping, Morgan Tanner handled the cattle and strove to improve the place. When he did go to town he wore a gun, but avoided places where there might be trouble. Several people made a point of telling him what Dunn had done to the Powell boys, and he knew they all expected a showdown between Dunn and himself.

Yet none of the Dunn riders appeared, and as long as he was left alone, Tanner was satisfied. The sun came out hotter each day, and the sky was cloudless. Wiley Dunn rode his sorrel out on the range beside his worried foreman. "What do you think, Ollie? Is the range all as bad as this?"

"There's places that are better. Back up in the breaks and in the deepest canyons. The water holes haven't slacked off too much yet, except that one down to Spur. That's gone dry."

There was silence, and Herndon asked cautiously, "Boss? D' you reckon we might sell a few head? Ease up on the grass a mite?"

Wiley Dunn stiffened. "No. Anyway, the price is off. We'd lose money to sell now."

Ollie Herndon said nothing. Gunman he might be, but he was also a cattleman. It was hard to sell when prices were down, yet better to sell now while they had beef on their bones than to let them lose weight. But he knew better than to make suggestions. Wiley Dunn had always had a fixation on numbers.

"If we had that Lonetree place it would help," he suggested. "You give me the word and I'll tackle Tanner."

Dunn waited while a man might have counted ten, staring out over the long brown miles of his range. He was wishing this affair had never come up. The expression in the eyes of Tanner's pretty wife had hurt him more than he would have admitted to anyone. He had grown more sensitive, he reflected, as he grew older. And if he faced Tanner now there would be no telling the outcome. If he died, what good would all these vast acres be? And if Tanner died, what would become of that lovely girl?

"No," he said finally, "not yet."

He saw nothing of Tanner. Twice he rode up the valley, keeping well out of sight, and another time he rode along a ridge overlooking the place from a distance.

Lonetree was more lovely than he remembered it. There had always been water there, but now there were long, perfectly lined rows of planted crops, and over against the far side there was a field of alfalfa, or what seemed to be alfalfa.

Tanner was no fool. He had a good thing there. He stared at the hay. Yet that was a lot of feed for the stock he had . . . suspicion leaped into his mind. Had Tanner turned to rustling? Had he, like other nesters in the past, started stealing cattle?

Suppose he had a small herd of Hat cattle that he was secretly fattening? With sudden decision, Dunn turned away. This was the explanation. There could be no other.

In the stone house against the cliff Morgan Tanner looked across the table at his wife. "Honey, I've been thinking. If we had us a Jersey bull now, a right fine Jersey from good milk stock, we might cross-breed those heifers into better milkers in a few seasons."

Ann Tanner looked at him thoughtfully. "You want to use that money Uncle Fred left us? Is that it?"

"It's your decision. It's up to you and Johnny. He was your uncle."

"But he left it to all of us! What do you think, Johnny?"

"I've been thinking about it, Sis. Morg never spoke of it before, but it's been in my mind. There's a market for milk and butter down at Algosa. This country has plenty of beef."

"All right," Ann agreed. "Buy a bull whenever you can find one you want."

"I'll go into town tomorrow," he said.

Morgan Tanner reached town at ten the following morning, and a few minutes earlier Wiley Dunn, Ollie Herndon, and twelve Hat hands swept down on the Lonetree ranch. It had been shrewdly planned, for Ollie had been watching the ranch with glasses and had seen the boy ride off on some mission. Instantly he was down off the ridge and they were riding.

There was no one about when they rode into the yard. Dunn shouted and, white-faced, Ann Tanner came to the door. "Just what is it you want, Mr. Dunn? Have you taken to fighting women now?"

His face flushed but his jaw was set. "I'm fighting no one, but we've come to search the range! That damn no-good husband of yours has taken to rustling cows. We seen some of them."

"We have no cattle but our own! Now I am ordering you to get off this place at once!"

She turned quickly to grasp the shotgun, but Herndon leaped from his horse and caught the barrel as she was swinging it up. He wrenched it roughly from her hands. "Right purty, ain't you? Maybe you could do with a good man after we string up that husband of yours!"

She slapped him across the mouth and Herndon struck her. She had stepped back, but the blow caught her on the forehead and knocked her down.

"Ollie!" Dunn was white-faced with anger. "For God's sake, man! Get into your saddle now, and be damned quick about it. I'll have no man strike a woman in my presence!" He pointed. "Get into your saddle, do you hear?"

Turning to Ann he said, "Sorry, ma'am, but you shouldn't have reached for that gun."

"And let you steal our cattle. You're asking for trouble, Mr. Dunn. You don't know Morgan as I do. Morgan Turner's mother was a Lowry, from the Neuces country. You may remember what happened to the Fullers."

Wiley Dunn stared at her, shocked. Every detail of the twenty-five year feud was known to everybody in cattle country. The Fullers, or some people who called themselves that, had killed a Lowry boy in an argument over horses, and every Fuller had died.

Suddenly, with startling clarity, he remembered the scene from years before. He himself had witnessed the final shootout. He had been visiting in Texas, planning to buy cattle, and four of the Fuller outfit had cornered two Lowrys, Bill Lowry and some youngster of sixteen or seventeen. They had shot Bill Lowry in the back, and then the kid turned on them.

The boy had drawn as he turned, a flashing, beautifully timed draw. Ed Fuller caught the first bullet in his mid-section as the boy fired. Thirty seconds later the youngster was in the saddle, riding out of town, leaving three Fullers dead and another dying. Now, suddenly, the face of that boy merged with that of Morgan Tanner. Of course! That was why there had always been something disturbingly familiar about the man.

There was no turning back now. "I'll stay here, Pete. The rest of you scatter out and find the cattle. When you find them, drive them out here."

"Those are not your cattle. We bought and paid for them."

Ollie Herndon did not leave. "Boss, let me go get him. I want him."

"Don't be a fool!" Dunn was worried and his temper was short. "That's the sheriff's job."

He paused. "Anyway, you're not in his class. Morgan Tanner is the one they used to call the Lowry kid."

"Aw, I don't believe it! Why, that—!"

"Mr. Dunn is right," Ann Tanner replied, "and when he learns what you have done, he will kill you. I wish you would ride now. I wish you would leave the country before he finds you."

Herndon laughed. "Since when have you started carin' about me?"

"I don't care about you. You're a cheap, loud-mouthed braggart, and a coyote at heart. You've gotten away with a lot because you ride in Mr. Dunn's shadow. I just do not want my husband to have to kill another man."

As they drove the cattle away, Ann looked after them, heartsick with worry and fear. Johnny appeared from the trees. "I seen 'em, Sis, but I didn't know what to do. I figured I'd better ride to town after Morg."

"No," she was suddenly thinking clearly, "you stay here and don't let them burn us out. I'll ride into town and see Sheriff Collins."

While Johnny was saddling her horse she hastily changed, fixed her hair, and got some papers from the strongbox.

Collins was shocked. "Ma'am, you can't do this! You can't arrest Dunn for stealin'! Why, he's the biggest cattleman in these parts!"

"Nevertheless, I have sworn out a warrant for his arrest, and I want you to come with me." She showed him the bill of sale for the cattle. "He has driven these cattle from my place, taking them by force, and Ollie Herndon struck me." She indicated the bruise on her brow.

"Sheriff, my husband is a Lowry. I want Wiley Dunn behind bars before my husband finds him."

"Just what happened out there, ma'am?" Reluctantly, he got to his feet. "Is that right? Is Morg the one they called the Lowry kid?"

At her assent, he started for the door. "You come along, ma'am, if you will. I don't want any killing here if it can be helped."

The Lowry kid was credited with nine men in all, but locally Morgan Tanner had been a quiet, reserved man, well-liked in the area, and always peaceful. Yet Collins knew the type. The West was full of them. Leave them alone and they were solid, quiet men who worked hard, morning until night; push them the wrong way and all Hell would break loose.

Suddenly Tanner was in the door. "Ann? What's wrong? I thought I saw you come in here." Then, "What's happened to your head?"

He listened, his face without expression, but as he turned to the door, Collins said, "Morg? Leave this to the law."

"All right. Except for Ollie. I'll take care of him."

"You're well liked around here, Morg. You want to spoil that by killing a man?"

"I won't kill him unless I have to. I'll just make him wish he was dead."

Wiley Dunn was talking with Ollie Herndon on the porch when Sheriff Collins, Morgan Tanner, and Ann rode into the ranch yard. By then there was a livid bruise where she had been struck.

"Dunn," Collins spoke apologetically, "I've got a warrant for your arrest. You and Ollie there. For rustlin'."

Ollie was watching Tanner. The expression in his eyes was almost one of hunger. "You huntin' me?"

"Pull in your neck," Tanner said calmly, "you'll have your turn."

Dunn's face was flushed with anger. "You'd arrest *me*? For *rustling*?"

"That's right," Collins said. "Mrs. Tanner has a bill of sale for those cattle you drove off. She bought 'em from the Bar Seven. Paid cash for 'em."

Dunn was appalled. "Look, this is a mistake. I thought—!"

"The trouble is that you didn't think at all," Tanner cut him off. "You've let yourself get so fat-headed and self-centered you didn't think at all.

"Dunn, all I've ever wanted from you is peace. You've no legal right to any of that range you hold. You've used it and misused it. Right now you're destroying the range with five thousand more cattle than the grass will carry.

"If you want to know the truth, Dunn, I've given serious thought to sending word back to Texas for two dozen friends of mine to come in and settle on your range. They'd file on it legally, and they are fighters. You'd be lucky to keep the house you live in."

"Tanner, maybe I've been some kind of a blind fool, but you wouldn't want to press those charges, would you? I might be able to beat your case, but I'd look the fool. You name the damages, and I'll pay. That all right with you, Sheriff?"

Collins waved a hand. "If Tanner drops his charges I'll say no more."

Morgan Tanner looked at Dunn and could find no malice in his heart. All that had been washed away back on the Neuces. He wanted only peace now, and Ann.

"No more trouble about Lonetree?"

"No more trouble. That's decent of you, Tanner. You had me over a barrel."

Herndon swore. "Boss? What's come over you? Knucklin' under to this plow-jockey? I'd see myself in—!"

His voice broke off and he started to draw as Tanner turned.

Tanner's draw was smooth and much faster. His first shot broke Ollie's arm at the elbow, spinning him half around. A second shot notched his ear, and as Ollie's other hand grabbed at the bloody ear, another bullet cut the lobe on the remaining ear.

Herndon turned and began to run clumsily. Tanner walked after him, gun poised. "You start riding, Herndon, and if you ever show up in this country again, I'll kill you.

"You aren't a tough man. You wouldn't make a pimple on a tough man's neck. You're a woman-beater. Now hit your saddle and get out of here."

Deliberately, he turned his back and walked to his own horse. He mounted, then glanced at the sheriff. "Thanks, Collins."

As Ann rode to him he looked around. "Have your boys drive those heifers back, Dunn. And drop around yourself some time, for supper."

Further along the road he said, "You know, that man Dunn might make a good neighbor. He's pig-headed, but in his place I might have been just as bad. Anyway, what a man needs in this country is good neighbors."

Then he added, "We'd better hurry. Johnny's apt to be worried, holdin' the fort there by himself."

When they rode into the yard Johnny came out from the house, a rifle in the hollow of his arm. At last it was sundown on the Lonetree.

LONG HENRY THOMPSON

He came to Montana from Texas with a herd of Rocking H cattle, and took a riding job with the NbarN. He was a tall, quiet man who was known to have killed three men somewhere back down the trail.

Long Henry carried a six-shooter from which the trigger and trigger-guard had been filed, and the gun was fired by simply pulling back the hammer and releasing it. The style, in some areas, was known as "slip-shooting." He carried his gun in a holster mounted on a swivel fastened to his belt, and usually he fired it by simply tilting the gun. He was amazingly accurate.

It was said he was one-quarter Cherokee, and he looked it. He drank little, smoked rarely, and tried to avoid trouble, yet somewhere along the line he had killed another man. Then came the trouble with George Denman, the NbarN camp cook.

Denman was a large, powerful man, heartily disliked, according to the NbarN hands, by everyone who knew him. His manner was deliberately obnoxious under normal conditions, and when drinking he became more so.

On the night in question Long Henry walked into Charlie Hanson's saloon with several other cowhands, to find Denman drinking at the bar.

Present also was another cowboy whom they all knew, named Wasson or Watson. He was a harmless, good-natured drunk, who invariably drank more than was good for him. On this night Denman was buying him drinks, then shoving him around just to see him fall, or spinning him, then laughing as the smaller man tumbled to the floor. It was an ugly spectacle made worse by a sudden spin that sent Watson crashing into the stove. Falling, his head hit the wood-box, inflicting a nasty cut.

As he lay there Denman threw a glass of whiskey in his eyes and said, "There! That should stop the bleeding!"

Long Henry walked across the room and lifted Watson from the floor and seated him on a chair. Then he wiped the drunken man's face, wiping away the whiskey and the blood. Then he turned to Denman and said, "I guess that will be enough of that for tonight, George."

Denman demanded, "Who the Hell are you, butting into my affairs?"

"I think you know who I am, George. I am just telling you to lay off this man."

Long Henry returned to the bar, finished his drink, and walked out.

Denman left Watson alone, but after leaving the saloon he went from one to another, muttering threats against Thompson.

The following morning, after loudly demanding where Long Henry was, Denman mounted his horse and was riding down the street when he saw Long Henry coming toward him. When about thirty feet apart, Denman pulled up and Long Henry also stopped.

Denman said, "I've got you right where I want you, Thompson!" And reached for his Winchester, which he carried butt-forward on the left side of his horse.

As the rifle slid from its scabbard, Long Henry tilted his six-shooter and fired. Denman stiffened, started to draw the rifle free, when Long Henry's second shot hit him. He let go of the rifle and fell into the street.

The first shot hit him just above the heart, the second in the throat.

Long Henry walked on down to Hanson's and said, "Will somebody notify the sheriff in Miles City? I have just killed George Denman."

It was September 24th, 1894.

JACKSON OF HORNTOWN

Horntown belonged to the desert. Whatever claim man had once had upon it had yielded to the sun, the wind and the blown sand. A double row of false-fronted buildings faced a dusty street into which the bunchgrass and sagebrush ventured. It had become a byway for an occasional rabbit or coyote, or the rattlers that had taken refuge in the foundations of The Waterhole, a saloon in which water had rarely been served.

A solitary burro wandered like a gray ghost among the weather-beaten, abandoned buildings.

To the east and west, craggy ridges of ugly red rock exposed their jagged crests to the sky. To the north, the narrow valley tapered away to a mere gully down which a dim trail led the unwary to that sink of desolation that was Horntown. To the south the valley widened into the Black Rock Desert. There were few trees and less water.

Had there been a watcher in the ghastly emptiness of the lifeless ridges he might have seen a lone horseman riding up the trail from the desert.

He rode a long-legged buckskin, which shambled wearily through the sagebrush, and even the sight of the ghost town failed to awaken any spark in either man or horse.

The watcher, had there been one, could have determined from the way the man rode that he was riding to a known destination. All the way across the waterless waste he had ridden as to a goal, and that in itself meant something.

99

For Horntown was a forgotten place, slowly giving itself back to the desert from which it had come. It had lived wildly, desperately, and it had died hard in a red-laced flurry of gunshots and powder smoke. The bodies of those who fell had been left where they had fallen, and the survivors had simply gone away and no one among them had looked back. Horntown was finished, and they knew it well.

Yet the sun-browned man with the bloody bandage on his head had kept his trail to Horntown; through all that broken country he had deviated by no more than a few feet from the direction he had chosen.

The red-rimmed gray eyes that occasionally stared back over the trail behind held no hint of mercy or kindness. They were the eyes of a man who had looked at life over a gun barrel, a man who had lived the hard, lawless way, and expected to die as he had lived.

It was fitting that he rode to Horntown, for the place had bred many such men. It had begun over a hundred years earlier, when a west-bound gold-seeker decided he had gone far enough. It died its first death two years later because the founder owned a horse, and a passing stranger needed a horse.

Jack Horn died with a gun in his hand. Seven months later a Mexican named Montez moved into the abandoned buildings and opened a saloon. He combined selling bad whiskey with robbing casual travellers until he chose the wrong man and died on his door-step. It was after that the first Jackson came to town.

Enoch Jackson was from Tennessee. Tall, leather-tough, and rawboned, he stopped in Horntown with his six sons, and the heyday of the town came into being.

It is a curious thing that no matter how sparse the vegetation or how remote the place, how difficult the problem of materials, a man who wants a drink will make one. The Jacksons had always had whiskey, and they had always made their own. They drank their own product, but drank it sparingly. Once set up in Horntown they drank even more sparingly for, of course, they alone knew the ingredients.

No one ever guessed and few asked what the whiskey was made from, but it fed fire into the veins of a hardy brood who turned the country to the south into a whirlwind of evil with their gunfighting, rustling, and hold-ups.

For fifty years the small Hell that was Horntown was ruled by Enoch and his powerful son, Matt Ben Jackson. A roving gunman, sore and hunting trouble, sent Enoch to his final pay-off with a bullet in his skull, and then died with Matt Ben's bullet just two hours later. He died where Matt Ben caught up with him, right where the valley of Horntown opened into the Black Rock Desert.

After that Matt Ben ran the show at Horntown with his brother, FireHat Jackson, as his lieutenant.

Several months later Sheriff Star Redman rode to Horntown with a posse of thirty men. They never reached their destination, but when the survivors rode home there were four empty saddles, and five men carried Jackson lead, to be removed later.

Redman was not of a yielding breed, and he had been elected to do a job. He returned, and on the fourth attempt the final bloody battle was fought. Star Redman had sworn he'd bring an end to Horntown or never return. There were twenty-six men in that last posse, and only seven of them returned unscathed. Several were buried in Horntown, and two died on the way back.

Behind them only one man remained alive, Matt Ben himself. Forty, tough, and badly wounded, he watched the last of the attackers ride away. Then, like a cornered rattler, he crawled back to The Waterhole and poured himself a drink.

A month later a wandering prospector found him dead on the floor, his gun in his hand. Matt Ben had amputated his own foot and shot himself when apparently dying of blood poisoning.

Searching the town, the prospector, who knew Horntown well, found the bodies of all the Horntown bunch but one. That one was FireHat. Or rather, all but two, for with FireHat had vanished Matt Ben the Younger.

"They'll come back," Sheriff Star Redman said bitterly, yet half in admiration. "He's a Horntown Jackson, and he'll be back. What I can't understand is why he ran away in the first place."

"Them Jacksons are feuders, Sheriff," the prospector reminded. "When FireHat left he took young Matt Ben with him, and he was only six and too young to fight."

"Maybe so," Redman admitted. "It could be he wanted to save him for seed."

FireHat Jackson died alone, ten years later, down in Sonora. The word drifted back to Webb City, sixty miles south of Horntown. Star Redman took the news with a strange light in his eyes. "Sonora, eh? How did he die?"

"Rurales surrounded him. He took eight of them along for company."

Redman spat. "You just know it! Them Jacksons never die alone. If one of 'em has a gun he'll take somebody along!"

"Well," somebody commented, "that ends the Horntown bunch. Now we can rest easy."

"Don't be too sure," Redman warned. "Matt Ben the Younger is somewhere around."

"But he wasn't one of the old bunch, Sheriff. He was too young to have it matter much. He won't even remember Horntown."

Star Redman shifted his tobacco in his jaws, chewed, then spat. "He was a Horntown Jackson!" He spat again. "You'll see. He'll be back."

"Sometimes, Star," the old storekeeper commented, "I think you almost wish he'd come back."

Redman had started toward the door, and now he turned. "He was one of the old breed. I'd rather he rode for the law, but say what you like about them Horntown Jacksons, they were *men!*"

The lone horseman slowed the yellow horse to a shambling trot, then to a walk. The buildings of Horntown were just ahead. He slid the Winchester from its boot. With his rifle across the saddle in front of him, he rode slowly up the one street of Horntown.

There were no more than twenty buildings still standing. The nearest was a gray, wind-battered house, and beyond were several shacks and corrals. Then the great, rambling old structure with its faded sign:

The Waterhole.

The rider of the yellow horse with the black tail and mane rode up the empty street. Here and there tumbleweeds had lodged. Sand had drifted like drifts of snow, doors hung on sagging hinges, creaking dismally in the wind. At one side of The Waterhole the run-off from the roof had worn a deep gully.

A spot of white at the corner of a building caught his eyes. It was a human skull, white and bleached. Grimly, he studied it. "More than likely he was one of my uncles," he said aloud.

He swung down in front of The Waterhole and tied the buckskin to the old hitching rail. His boots had a hollow, lonesome sound on the boardwalk. He opened the door and walked in.

Dust and cobwebs hung over everything. The chairs and tables remained much as they must have been when the fight ended. A few poker chips were scattered about, an empty bottle stood on a table, another on the bar beside a tipped-over shot-glass. Propped against the bar was a skeleton, rifle beside it, gun-belt still hanging to the lank white bones. One foot was missing.

Slowly the man uncovered his head. "Well, Pa, you died hard, but you died game."

Outside he went to where the spring was, the reason why old Jack Horn had stopped in the first place. Crystal-clear water still ran from the rocks and trickled into a natural basin, then trickled off down through the rocks and into the wash, where it lost itself in a small cluster of cottonwoods and willows.

He filled his canteen first, as any sensible man would, then he drank, and, removing the bloody bandage, carefully bathed his head where a bullet had cut a furrow. Then, still more carefully, he washed his hair.

He led the buckskin to water, then picketed him on a small patch of grass he remembered from the days when he had played there as a youngster.

Inside the saloon he found dishes, washed them, and, working at the fireplace, prepared a rough meal.

He was digging a grave for his father's bones when he heard a faint sound, then another. His gun slid easily into his hand and he waited, listening to the slow steps, shambling, hesitant. Then a long gray head appeared around the corner.

Matt Ben holstered his gun, then he climbed out of the

grave and held out his hand to the burro. "Hi, Zeke! Come here!"

At the sound of the familiar name the burro's head lifted, and the scent of this man apparently touched a chord of memory, but still he hesitated. Matt Ben called again and again, and slowly the old burro walked toward him.

"It's all right, Zeke. It's just a Jackson, come home at last. I'm glad you waited."

Three days later Pierce Bowman walked into the sheriff's office in Webb City. "Wire for you, Star. Looks like you were right. Matt Ben's on his way home."

"He's already here," Redman commented dryly. "Tim Beagin came by there day before yesterday. Saw smoke in The Waterhole's chimney.

"I didn't plan to bother him. Seems sort of natural, havin' a Jackson out there, but this here wire changes matters. I got to go get him."

"You takin' a posse?"

"No. Just me. If he's a Jackson we'd never get nigh him. Them Jacksons always could smell a posse ten mile off."

"What do they want him for?"

"Sheriff over at Carson tried to take him and he wouldn't go, said he was just ridin' through. The sheriff made a mistake then. He reached for his gun, and Matt Ben put him out of commission."

"Jacksons always could shoot. How d' you figure to take him, Star?"

"Darned if I know. I think I'll just go talk to him." He paused. "You know something, Bowman? Nobody ever did try just talkin' to a Jackson. They always went for them with guns and ropes. Maybe somebody should have tried talkin' a long time ago."

Star Redman took the trail to Horntown carrying no pleasant thoughts. He had no desire, at his age, to shoot it out with a Horntown Jackson. Once, when he was younger, he might have felt otherwise, but time had tempered his courage with wisdom. The Jacksons, like himself, had been products of their times, but not really bad men. They never killed except when firing at an equal in open combat.

There had been, he remembered, a certain something on their side. His job was to arrest young Matt Ben, and of course that was what he must do. This young Jackson might be different, but again he might not. The Jackson blood was strong.

He remembered very well the time the shooting ended at Horntown. "I think he's dead," somebody commented. "Shouldn't we go in and find out?"

An old-timer in the posse looked around. "You want to go in, you go. Me, I wouldn't go in if you offered me your ranch!"

Star Redman knew the hills. He believed he knew them better than young Matt Ben, and in his knowledge he saw his chance—to get close without arousing suspicion. He glanced skyward. "Smells like snow," he said to himself. "Time for it, too."

Young Matt Ben was thinking the same thing. He began gathering wood and scrap lumber, which he piled alongside The Waterhole. He began making repairs in the room he expected to use, and also in the stable where he could keep the buckskin.

In the lower meadow, just beyond the willows, he found a fine stand of hay, and began mowing it with a scythe he sharpened in the blacksmith shop. It was time for snow to fall, and if he expected to winter at Horntown he had best be ready for it.

He enjoyed working with his hands. He repaired the door, making it a tight fit. He found the old livery stable had almost fallen in, and rescued some good-sized timbers for burning. His father's house was down the street, and there was a good stack of wood there, enough for a winter.

He avoided the thought of food. He had enough for three or four days, with care. He worked from dawn until dark mowing hay, and the sun would cure it. Yet he would have to get it in before snow fell.

Here and there he found where passersby had camped. Prospectors or sheepmen, perhaps some drifting cowhand.

Old Zeke hung around, wary, but liking the company. Several times he tried to entice the old burro to come into the stable, but he was too wary, and would have none of it. Finally, by dropping bunches of grass, he got him to go inside.

He left the door open but Zeke was liking the buckskin's company.

"The last of the Jacksons!" he said aloud. "Me and a jackass!"

He studied the sky grimly. It was surely going to snow.

Twenty miles north and east was the hideout of Stony Budd. The Budd gang had looted two banks, run off a bunch of fine saddle stock, and holed up over there.

"Come along, Matt," Budd suggested, "that's old Jackson country. We could use you up there."

"Not me. I'm through with the outlaw trail. From here out I'm ridin' a straight trail. If they'll let me," he added.

He meant it, too. There was food, warmth, and security up there with Stony Budd. All he needed to do was to saddle the buckskin and head for the hills.

To stay here might mean to invite trouble. People would learn a Jackson had returned, and he would have to live down a hard name. Well, it was high time a Jackson did live it down. Old Enoch would have agreed with that. Times had changed. Even old FireHat had told him so.

He would have had no trouble but for that sheriff in Carson. The man had tried to arrest him without reason. The sheriff, wanting to build a reputation, figured arresting a Horntown Jackson would convince the voters. Matt Ben had been about to go along with it until something in the man's snaky eyes changed his mind.

"Tell me what you want me for, and I'll go. Otherwise I am settin' right here."

"I'm arresting you on suspicion," the sheriff had said. "Now cut the palaver and come along."

"Suspicion of what?"

"It don't make no matter. You come along."

Matt Ben hesitated, then surrendered his belt gun. "Now, damn you," the sheriff said. "Here's where I kill me a Jackson!"

He had failed to notice the open button on the front of Matt Ben's shirt, and when he dropped his hand for his gun, Matt Ben shot him. Then he retrieved his own six-shooter, mounted his buckskin, and rode out of town.

Matt Ben was frying bacon over the fire when he heard a

light step. The frying pan was in his left hand, a fork in his right. For an instant, he froze.

"Don't try it, son," Star Redman said. "I don't want to kill you."

"Then you're different from that sheriff back in Carson," Matt Ben said. "That was just what he planned to do."

He glanced at the tall man standing inside the door. He was a lean, rangy man with quizzical gray-blue eyes and a white, drooping mustache.

"I suppose you're Star Redman," he said. "Come up to the fire. The coffee's hot."

Redman, holding his gun steady, stepped over and slid the guns from Jackson's holsters.

"Sorry, Jackson. I knew you were here and didn't plan on botherin' you until I got word from Carson."

"Sit down and we'll eat. I'm runnin' shy on grub, but we'll manage." He looked up. "FireHat said you were a fair man, Sheriff, and that you were a fighter."

Redman sat down opposite Jackson and studied him as he prepared the meal. He was a well-built man, obviously strong, with all the marks of a rider. A glance at his hands showed evidence of hard work.

"Morning is soon enough to start, isn't it, Redman?" Matt Ben asked. "This has been a long day."

"We'll start tonight," Redman said. "I don't want to spend the night here." He smiled. "No, I'm not worried about ghosts. It's snow. There's a feel of it in the air."

"FireHat told me about this country," Matt Ben said, "and he said Horntown was rightly mine. Is that true?"

"It is," Redman admitted. "Enoch proved up on a claim and so did seven of the others. Actually, you own all the water for miles around, and what range you don't own lies between pieces you do own. I've seen it all on a map. Old Enoch was no damn fool."

Matt Ben served the bacon and the sourdough bread and refilled their cups. So this was the end of the dream! He had thought to return here, to whip the place into some kind of shape and by hard work to establish himself as a peaceful rancher. If it had not been for that sheriff in Carson—

There was always Stony Budd.

A fire quickened within him. Well, why not? He had the name, so he might as well take the game. It was a long way to Webb City, and many things might happen, particularly if it began to snow.

The old sheriff might be a fighter, but with all his posses he couldn't crack the Jacksons, and he would not crack this one now.

He would need a gun.

Well, he had planned for this, knowing it might happen, although it was trouble with Stony and his crowd that he expected.

He was not fooling himself about Budd. The outlaw leader wanted him because he was good with a gun, but even more because he was afraid Matt Ben might start operations of his own. Stony Budd had his own reputation. He was rumored to have killed five men in gun battles.

Matt Ben, expecting trouble, had two guns hidden out. Two on which he could depend. There was a six-shooter hidden under a canvas in the manger where he stabled the buckskin. There was another in the folds of his slicker.

Outside the wind was picking up. They could hear it growing stronger. It would be a bad night.

"We'd better get movin'," Redman said, pushing back his plate.

Matt Ben got up and began tossing things into his war bag, then turned to pick up his slicker. As he stooped for it Redman spoke.

"If'n I was to have a hide-out gun," he spoke casually, "I'd be likely to have it hidden in my slicker."

Matt Ben straightened, the folded slicker in his hands. After all, Star Redman had killed several of his relatives, and if right now he were to leap to one side and shoot from the slicker he'd have no worse than an even break. Then he realized he did not want to kill the old man. He did not even want to hurt him. And on the trail he would have his chance. A chance to slip away in the storm.

"Seems you've outguessed me, Mr. Redman," he said, "because I surely do have a gun here."

Star took the gun from the open folds of the slicker. His eyes were thoughtful. "You could've taken a chance, son. You might have nailed me."

He smiled. "Of course, I was ready, but you can never tell. It's a chancy game, son."

Watched by the sheriff, he went into the stable to get the buckskin. When in the stall and momentarily beyond view of Redman, Matt Ben slipped the manger gun into the front of his shirt. He had already donned the slicker as protection from the cold wind, and the gun made no bulge that could be seen through its looseness.

Straddling the yellow horse he spoke to Zeke. "You stay inside where it's warm," he whispered. "I'll be back or send the sheriff to open up for you when the storm's gone. I'm still planning to stay here in Horntown with you."

At the last minute, worried that the burro might be forgotten and starve, he left the door ajar. He rode out of town, Star Redman following. Once, he looked back. The old gray burro was walking after them into the desert, and into the storm.

Star Redman stared at the sky, obviously worried. Yet they had been riding for an hour when the first snowflake fell. Then there was another, and suddenly the air was white with them.

"We'll keep goin'," Redman said, "maybe it won't be so bad."

They both knew what it might mean to be caught out in the wastes of the Black Rock in a blizzard, and the snow was falling thickly now. There was little wind, and that was a blessing. They rode on, Matt Ben watching for his chance. If he could get even fifty yards away he could not be seen.

The horses moved more slowly. Matt Ben glanced back. Their tracks were covered almost as soon as they stepped out of them. The wind was rising. It blew a sudden gust, almost sucking the air from his lungs.

"Gettin' mighty bad!" Redman shouted.

Matt Ben was almost imperceptibly widening the gap between them. Just a little more and he would be completely obscured by falling snow.

He let the yellow horse find his way into a deep gully. Here the snow had drifted, and he let the buckskin pick his way with care down the steep side of the ravine. A misstep here and a horse could break a leg.

Glancing around, he instantly went into action. The sheriff was still out of sight beyond the lip of the ravine. Turning the yellow horse, he touched spurs to him and raced away up the ravine. After a momentary spurt he let the yellow horse take his own speed. Behind him he heard a shout, then another.

Matt Ben Jackson rode on. He reined the buckskin to a stop, listening. There was no sound but the wind, and his trail was already blotting out. He was free again.

When he had ridden another mile he found a place where he could climb the horse out of the ravine. The minute his head cleared the top he felt a blast of icy wind which struck him like a blow. They had been drifting ahead of the wind when going toward Webb City; now he must face it.

Horntown was the safest place now. There was fuel and there was shelter from the wind and snow. He could last out the storm, then head for Stony Budd's and then up to Wyoming.

The snow was falling heavier now, the wind rising. It was to be a bad storm. He turned the yellow horse toward the trail down which they had come; some of the route had been sheltered from the worst of the wind. He doubted the old sheriff would attempt a return in this storm. He would wait until it was over, and then come with a posse. Matt Ben knew his escape had been the merest fluke.

He cut their trail near a rocky shoulder which offered some protection from the wind, and dismounted to rest the buckskin. Then he saw their tracks. Here, sheltered from the wind, they had neither filled with snow nor blown away. And there, over the tracks of his horse and that of the sheriff, were the unmistakable hoofprints of the old gray burro. It was strange the storm had not turned it back.

Matt Ben stared at the tracks, swearing under his breath. From where he now stood it was at least forty-five miles to Webb City, and that old gray burro, the last survivor of Horntown, would never make it.

He would die out here on the snow-covered desert. The tracks indicated the old burro was lagging far behind, as the horse tracks had begun to fill before the sharper burro tracks were made.

"Matt Ben," he told himself disgustedly, "you're a fool for what you're thinking." Yet even as he said it he knew he was going back after the old burro. He was going to get Zeke and take him back to Horntown. It wouldn't be right to let the old fellow die out there alone. Around the town, with shelter, he might live several years.

He mounted again and turned the buckskin back on the trail. It was somewhat sheltered in places, and occasional tracks remained. Several times he had to stop, judging the wind. He hoped it was holding to the north. It was a full hour later when he found the ravine where he had lost the sheriff.

Reining in, he took his six-gun from his shirt and thrust it behind his belt under the slicker. Then he felt his way down the steep trail.

When he reached the bottom Zeke was standing not a half-dozen yards away. Nearby, propped against the rock wall was Star Redman. His head was slumped on his chest and near him was a small pile of sticks beginning to be covered with snow. His horse stood a few feet to one side.

"What the devil?" Matt Ben scowled. For a moment he stood in the slowly falling snow and simply stared, filled with a great exasperation.

Zeke saw him first and lifted his head, ears canted forward. "It's all right, Zeke. Everything's all right."

Bending over the sheriff, he put a hand on his shoulder. Redman stirred, wincing sharply. Matt Ben looked down. Even under the snow he could see an odd twist to Redman's leg.

"What happened?"

"Hoss slipped comin' into the ravine. Fell with me, an' busted my leg. Guess I must've passed out as I was tryin' to build a fire." He looked up. "I yelled at you, but I guess you didn't hear."

Matt Ben straightened up, swearing mentally. He walked over to the sheriff's horse. The horse was sound. He led it over to Redman.

"I can't leave you here. I'll take you back to Horntown. It's closer."

Rousting around in the frozen brush, he found a couple of sticks and made a crude splint for the leg. Then he lifted the old man into the saddle. For a man of his frame he was surprisingly light. Matt Ben steadied him in the saddle. "Can you stick it? Damn it, Redman, you're too old a man to be livin' this kind of life."

The sheriff looked down at him. "I know, son, but what else can I do? I kept the peace in the country while all the others got rich in the cattle or sheep business. All of a sudden I was an old man who had nothing but a star and a reputation for doin' my job."

Matt Ben climbed into his own saddle after leading Redman's horse up the bank. "Come on, Zeke," he said, "you got to show Redman you're tough as he is. Let's go home."

It was slow going. The wind was an icy blast which stung their faces with frozen snow. The sheriff bowed his head into the wind and clung to the saddle-horn. He made no sound, but Matt Ben knew he was suffering.

A long time later Matt Ben dismounted and stamped his almost-frozen feet. He was cold all the way through. He swung his arms in a teamster's warming and walked around, rubbing the legs of the horses and of old Zeke, who stood patiently, as though he had lived all his life with men, when in fact he had run wild for years.

Mounting, he pushed on, followed by the others. From time to time he looked over his shoulder to see if they were still behind him.

They were riding right into the wind, and that should be right, but suppose the wind had shifted? Even if it shifted but little, it still might cause him to miss the canyon mouth and ride on into the endless wastes of the desert.

The horses were of little help, as neither was from Horntown. Their inclination was to turn their tails to the wind and drift, but in that direction there was at least fifty miles of empty, wind-swept desert.

He looked around at Zeke. The old gray burro stood a few yards away, almost at right angle to their route, staring back at him. On a hunch, he turned the buckskin toward the burro and, as if waiting for that very thing, Zeke walked off, quartering into the wind.

"Hope you know where you're goin' old fellow," Matt Ben muttered, "because I surely don't."

Zeke was obviously going somewhere. He walked steadily ahead, as though completely sure of his ground. What if the burro thought he was being herded in that direction? It was a risk he must take, but the old burro was desert-wise, and it stood to reason he would head for shelter.

Hours later, it seemed, half-frozen and numb with cold, the buckskin stumbled. Matt Ben, jerked from a half doze, looked up to see the gray burro walking straight at a jumble of unfamiliar rocks. Above the rocks, barely visible through the snow, towered a mountain. It might be one of the mountains behind Horntown!

Yet nothing was familiar. He swung down and, leading his horse, he plodded ahead. Suddenly the wind was gone. Looking up, he found the burro had led them into a rock-walled canyon. Plodding after the burro, his feet clumsy with cold, he found himself back in the wind again. He stopped, not believing what he saw.

There before him was a cluster of buildings covered with snow!

Zeke was walking straight ahead, for Zeke knew where he was going. He was returning to Horntown!

Two hours later, a fire roaring in the fireplace, Matt Ben handed another cup of scalding coffee to the sheriff. "Hadn't been for that old burro we'd have froze to death."

"Yes," Redman agreed, "and if you hadn't been goodhearted enough to worry about that burro, I'd be dead by now. You could have left me there, anyway."

"Huh?" Matt Ben stared at him sourly. "Now why the Devil would I do that? There wouldn't be anybody to fight with, then." He added a snowy log to the fire. "But you'd better get some help. You're too old for this sort of thing."

"How'd you happen to shoot that man in Carson?"

Matt explained. "He was fixin' to kill me. He wanted the name of killin' the last of the Jacksons of Horntown.

"The law has nothing against me but that. I've done a few

things I shouldn't have done but there's nothing anybody can prove, and nothing they've got me tied to. I was through with all that. Being on the dodge all the time is no life for a man."

"We might find witnesses," Redman said thoughtfully. "Maybe somebody saw it. Seems to me that somebody always sees things, even when we think nobody is around. If we could prove that was a fair shooting we could get you off. That officer had a bad reputation among us who knew him. He had the instincts of a bully, and used his badge for protection."

He tugged at his mustache. "Anyway, I'd say a man who would come back and help an officer who'd just taken him prisoner couldn't be all bad.

"Another thing. You're right about me gettin' on in years. I need help. I need a deputy who can use a gun when needed but isn't anxious to go around shooting folks."

Matt Ben went out into the storm and crossed to the stable. The two horses and the old burro were chewing methodically on the grass in their mangers, and they rolled their eyes at him when he came in.

The sheriff had carried a little grub and a lot of coffee, and with what Matt Ben had they could live out the storm.

Matt Ben walked over to Zeke and rubbed the old burro's back. "Zeke, you old gray devil. I think we Jacksons have come back to Horntown to stay."

He stood a moment, his hand resting on the burro. Outside the wind moaned around the eaves. It was cold out there, but the stable was snug and warm.

He went outside, closing the door carefully behind him, then, turning the top of his head into the wind, he crossed the street to The Waterhole.

At the door, half-sheltered from the wind, he looked back. Old Enoch had built well. The barn was old but it was strong against the wind.

Enoch had meant to sink roots here, to found a family. Well, it was up to him now, to Matt Ben Jackson the Younger.

TASCOSA

It was March 20, 1886, and four cowboys from the LS Ranch took a notion to ride into town to see the girls and have a few drinks. It was a notion they could well have ignored, for only one of them would ever ride back.

They were tough men, hired as much for their fighting ability as their skill in handling stock, or so it was said. They were Ed King, Fred Chilton, Frank Valley and John Lang.

When they rode past the Jenkins & Dunn Saloon Lem Woodruff left the porch and went inside, for Lem had good reason to expect trouble. The others stayed where they were.

Louis Bousman, the Catfish Kid, Tom and Charley Emory were there and none of them had good feelings about the four riders from the LS. It is very likely that the cowboys had come to town either looking for or expecting trouble.

It was a hot, sultry evening, and Jesse Sheets, who had been in Tascosa for about a year, decided to sleep in a room in back of his cafe where it was cooler. It was a decision he would not live to regret. He was a peaceful man, in no way involved in the troubles of town or range. He had a large family and a small business, which offered worries enough.

Women were also involved in the troubles, but basically it was the old story of nesters and small ranchers against the big cattlemen, and the LS was one of the big outfits. Lem Woodruff, however, had been Sally Emory's man, but she had thrown him over for Ed King. Lem had rebounded quickly, however,

115

and landed in the willing arms of Rocking-Chair Emma. Despite the fact that she had dropped him for Ed King, Sally was irritated by Lem's quick recovery, and haunted by the idea that maybe he had been planning just such a move. A rumor was around that she had been urging Ed King to kill Lem. Without a doubt, Lem Woodruff knew of the rumors.

Ed King was known as a tough man, with at least one killing behind him. He was known around Mobeetie and Fort Griffin as a dangerous man, and was a leader among the LS cowboys.

Shortly after arriving in town, he was walking by the Jenkins & Dunn Saloon with Sally Emory when King overheard a remark which he resented. Sending Sally along by herself, he turned back and started to enter the saloon, where the lights suddenly went out. Although the men on the porch were known to him, the sudden darkness could have given him no more than a quick glance of who was within.

He must have seen the flash at the instant the bullet hit him. Caught in mid-stride, he fell, dead before he hit the floor, his gun half-drawn. Who doused the light was never known, but it is likely that the last thing Ed King saw was Lem Woodruff holding a rifle.

With the report sounding in their ears, the men on the porch scattered, knowing very well what was to come. Someone, later surmised to have been Lem Woodruff, rushed from the saloon and fired another shot into King, to make sure he was dead.

John Lang, who had left Ed and Sally just before they reached the Jenkins & Dunn Saloon, turned back when he heard the comment from the darkness that had stopped Ed King.

He heard the shot, saw Ed King fall, and ran up the street to alert his companions. Guns drawn, they converged on the spot, and an instant's check told them Ed King was dead. Hearing a sound from behind the saloon, they rushed around into a blaze of gunfire.

In the area immediately behind the saloon five or six men had gathered, apparently concocting some plan for future action. Frank Valley opened fire as he charged into them. Emory was shot in the leg, Woodruff took two bullets in the body, but retreated into the saloon, holding his fire. Valley, poised for action, went after him and was shot dead.

Jesse Sheets, awakening from a sound sleep, blundered into the night to see what was happening, and was killed. Undoubtedly, whoever shot him saw the looming figure and simply fired. Fred Chilton, rising from behind a woodpile to fire, was hit by two bullets in the chest and fell.

John Lang, the only survivor, retreated up the street, firing. Right at that moment what he wanted most was a fast horse and the road to the LS line camp.

Sheriff Jim East, accompanied by a deputy, found Sheets dead, then came upon the bodies of Ed King and Frank Valley in the saloon, either in or near the front and back doorways.

The saloon was empty. Lem Woodruff, the Emorys, and the Catfish Kid had vanished into the night.

Conducting a swift search, East came upon Louis Bousman in bed, smoking a half-burned cigar. Jim East, who knew Bousman well, for they had ridden on posses together, said, "Always go to bed with your boots on, Louis?"

Bousman smiled, dusted ash from the dead cigar and replied, "I was just tired tonight, Jim. Would you believe it? I just dropped down on the bed and fell asleep!"

Charlie Emory was found, badly wounded. Lem Woodruff, in even worse shape, had gotten to the house of a friend, some distance away.

A bystander, emerging from a nearby store, pointed out the body of Chilton, behind the woodpile.

Four new graves were dug, three of them on Boot Hill, and two men seriously wounded.

It had been a hot night in old Tascosa.

THERE'S ALWAYS A TRAIL

H e sat on a bale of hay against the wall of the livery stable
and listened to them talk. He was a lean, leather-skinned
man with bleak eyes and a stubble of beard on his jaw. He was
a stranger in Pagosa, and showed no desire to get acquainted.

"It's an even bet he's already dead," Hardin said, "there
would be no reason to keep him alive once they had the
money."

"Dead or alive, it means we're finished! That was all the
money we could beg, borrow, or steal."

"Leeds was killed?" Hardin asked. He was a burly man with
a hard red face. Now his blue eyes showed worry. "Then he
can't tell us a thing!"

"That's just the trouble!" Caughey said. "We haven't a clue!
Salter starts to town from our ranch with our fifteen thousand
dollars and Bill Leeds along as body-guard. Leeds is dead, two
shots fired from his gun, and Salter is gone."

"It's a cinch Salter didn't take our money," Hardin said,
"because he would have shot Leeds down from behind. Salter
knew Leeds was good with a gun, and he'd never have taken a
chance."

"Jake Salter isn't that sort of man," Bailey protested. "He's a
good man. Dependable."

The stranger in the dusty black hat crossed one knee over
the other. "Anybody trailin' them?" His voice had a harsh,
unused sound.

119

Hardin glanced around, noticing him for the first time. "There isn't any trail. Whoever done it just dropped off the edge of the earth. We hunted for a trail. The body of Bill Leeds was lyin' on the road to town, and that was all there was!"

"There's always a trail, but you aren't going to get your money back if you stand around talkin' about it. Why not scout around? There's always some sign left."

"Hunt where?" Hunt asked irritably. "A man's got to have a place to start. There's no trail, I said!"

The stranger's eyes were bored but patient. Slowly, he got to his feet. "If I'd lost that money, I'd go after it." He turned on his heel and started along the street toward the Star Saloon.

"Wait a minute! Hold on there!" Cass Bailey said. "Hey! Come back here!"

The man turned and walked slowly back. The others were looking at Bailey, surprised. "What's your name, friend?" Bailey asked.

"There's places they've said I was right handy, so just call me that, Handy."

"All right, Handy. You've done some talking. You said if that was your money you'd go after it. Well, four thousand of that money happens to be mine, and it represents every head of beef that was fit to sell on the CB range. As of now, half that money is yours, if you can get it. You lost two thousand dollars in the holdup, so now we'll see whether you're going to find a trail or not."

Handy stuck his thumbs behind his belt. "You said if you lost that money you were through, finished. Is that right?"

"It ain't only me," Bailey said. "We're all through if we don't get our money back."

"All right, Bailey, I like the way you talk. I'll accept that two thousand on one consideration. If I get it back it buys me a full partnership in your CB range."

Hardin jumped up. "Well of all the—!"

Cass Bailey stood, feet apart, hands on his hips, staring at Handy. Obviously, the man was a rider. There was something about his hard assurance that Bailey liked.

"If you can get that money back, you've got yourself a deal."

"Find me a place to sleep," Handy said. "I'll be along in a few days."

Handy turned away and walked along to the Star Saloon and ordered a beer. He took a swallow of the beer then put the glass back on the bar.

"Too bad about Leeds," the bartender suggested. He was a lean, loose-mouthed man with straw-colored hair and watery eyes.

"Too bad about Salter, too. Probably they'll kill him. That will be hard on his family."

"Salter? He's got no family. At least none that anybody knows of."

"What about his woman?"

"You know about her, huh? From all I hear, Maria won't do any frettin'. That Maria, she's a case, Maria is. She sure had ol' Jake danglin'. He was all worked up over her. Every time he saw her he acted like he'd been kicked in the head."

"Maria? Is she over at Cherry Hill?"

"Cherry Hill? You must be thinkin' of somebody else. There's nobody like Maria! They tell me those Spanish are somethin' special. Never knew one, m'self."

Handy finished his beer and strolled outside. Cass Bailey was nowhere in sight, but Handy had no sooner appeared on the boardwalk than a storm descended upon him.

It was five feet, three inches of storm, and shaped to make disaster inviting. Ann Bailey. Her hair was red, and there was a sprinkling of freckles across her nose, and what were probably very lovely lips were drawn into a thin line as her boot heels clackity-clacked down the walk toward him.

"Listen, you! If you're the one who sold my dad a bill of goods and got him to give up half his ranch—! Why you no-good fish-eatin' crow-bait, I've a notion to knock your eyes out!"

"You've already done that, ma'am. But what's the trouble? Don't you want your money back?"

"Want it back? Of course, I want it back! But you've no right to talk my old man into any such deal as that! Besides, what makes you think you can get it back? Unless you're one of the outlaws who stole it!"

"Do you live on the ranch?" he asked mildly.

"Where else would I live? In a gopher hole?"

"Ain't no tellin', ma'am, although if you did, that gopher would feel mighty crowded. Still an' all, I can see where makin' my home on the CB might be right nice."

He stepped into the street and tightened the cinch on the evil-eyed buckskin who stood at the rail looking unpleasant.

"Ma'am, I like my eggs over, my bacon not quite crisp, and my coffee black and strong. You just be expectin' me now!"

Handy reined the buckskin around and loped away down the street, followed by some language that, while not profane, certainly made profanity unnecessary.

"Spirit," he told the buckskin, "that's what I like!" The buckskin laid back his ears and told himself, 'You just wait until the next frosty morning, cowhand, and I'll show you spirit!'

Hondo could have doubled for Pagosa, except that the Star Saloon was two doors further along the street and was called the Remuda, probably because they played so much stud.

The bartender was fat, round, and pink-cheeked. He was also, by looks and sound, very definitely an Irishman. "I'm not one of the fighting Irish," he said, "I'm one of the loving Irish, and I like the girls when they're fair, fat, and forty."

"You wouldn't like Maria, then," Handy commented. "I hear she's slim, dark, and twenty."

"Don't you get any ideas, cowboy. Maria's spoken for. Her time's taken. Anyway, from a mere sideline observer I'd guess that twenty was a shade closer to thirty. But she's spoken for."

"I heard about Salter," Handy said.

The bartender's smile was tolerant, the smile of one who knows. "That's what Salter thinks! Maria is Buck Rodd's girl. She lets Salter hang around because he buys her things, and that's all it amounts to.

"Believe me," the bartender took a quick glance around the empty room and lowered his voice, "if she's smart she won't try any funny business with Buck Rodd!"

"Heard of him," said Handy, who hadn't, "and that crowd he runs with."

"You'll be liable to hear more before the day's over, if you stay in town. Buck rode in last night with that whole crowd,

Shorty Hazel, Wing Mathy, Gan Carrero, and some other gent."

"That's enough for me," Handy said, finishing his beer. "I never heard of Maria. I'll stick to blondes when I'm in Hondo."

The bartender chuckled agreement and Handy went outside, where he found a chair and settled down to doze away what remained of the afternoon.

"The trouble with folks," Handy mused, "is they make it hard for themselves. A man leaves more than one kind of a trail. If you can't find the tracks that shows where he went you can nearly always back-track him to where he came from. Then it usually comes down to one of them 'searches la fammy' deals like that tenderfoot was explainin' down at El Paso. If you're huntin' a man, he said, look for the woman. It makes sense, it surely does."

Three horsemen fast-walked their horses to the hitchrail near his own, and swung down. The slim, dark one would probably be Carrero, the one with the short leg would be Wing Mathy, and the one with the hard face and sand-colored hair would be Shorty Hazel.

Handy built himself a cigarette, innocently unaware of the three. The two guns he wore took their attention, but he did not look around when one of them muttered something to the others.

Wing Mathy stepped up on the boardwalk. "Hey? Ain't you from the Live Oak country?"

"I might be," Handy said, "but I could be from Powder River or Ruby Hills. So might you, but I ain't askin'."

Mathy smiled. "I ain't askin', friend. It's just that you looked familiar."

The three went inside and as the door swung to, Handy heard Wing say, "I've seen that gent somewhere. I know I have!"

Handy looked down at the cigarette. He rarely smoked, and didn't really want this one. It had been something to keep his fingers busy. He dropped it to the boardwalk, careful it did not go through to the debris below, and rubbed it out with his boot-toe.

He was on the trail of something, but just what he was not

sure. Right about now Buck Rodd was probably seeing Maria.
At least, he might be.

Most people, when they went to chasing outlaws, spent too
much time wearing horses out. He found it much more simple
to follow the trails from a chair, even though he'd spent the
largest part of his life in a saddle.

What had become of Jake Salter? That was the next problem,
and just where was the money?

Jake Salter was out of his skull over Maria, and Maria was
Buck Rodd's girl. Jake Salter, trying to impress her with how
big a man he was, might have mentioned carrying all that
money. She would surely have told Buck Rodd. There is very
little, after all, that is strange about human behavior. All the
trails were blazed long, long ago.

Handy led his horse to the livery stable. Livery stables, he
had discovered, were like barber shops. There was always a lot
of talk around, and if a man listened he could pick up a good
deal. He led the buckskin inside, bought it a night's keep for
two bits, and began giving the surprised horse a rubdown.

The buckskin was a little uncertain as to the proper reaction
to such a procedure. Upon those past occasions when he had
been rubbed down it was after a particularly gruelling time on
the trail, but on this day he had done practically nothing. He
was gratified by the rubdown, but felt it would only be in
character to bite, kick, or act up somehow. However, even
when preoccupied, as he was now, Handy rarely gave him
opportunities. The buckskin relaxed, but the idea stayed with
him.

For two days Handy had idled about the livery stable in
Pagosa before coming here, so he knew that Salter owned a
little spread over on the Seco. The brand was the Lazy S. A
few minutes now sufficed to show there was no Lazy S horse in
the stable, but he waited, and he listened.

As night settled down he saddled the buckskin again and
strolled outside. The night was softly dark, the stars hanging so
low it seemed a tall man might knock them down with a stick.
Handy sat down on a bench against the stable wall. A lazy-
fingered player plucked a haphazard tune from a piano in the
saloon up the street. Occasionally the player sang a few bars, a

plaintive cow country song born some centuries ago on the plains of Andalusia, in far-off Spain. Nothing stirred. Once there was a burst of laughter from the saloon, and occasionally he could hear the click of poker chips.

Down the street a door opened, letting a shaft of lamplight into the darkness. A big man swaggered out. The door closed, and Handy could hear the jingle of spurs and boot heels on the boardwalk, and then, in the light from over the swinging doors of the Remuda, Handy saw a big man enter. He wore a black hat and a black shirt, and his handle-bar mustache was sweeping and black. Buck Rodd.

Handy arose and rubbed a finger along the stubble of beard. It was no way in which to call on a lady. Still . . . he walked down the opposite side of the street from the saloon and turned in at the gate from which Rodd had emerged.

Hesitating to step up on the porch, he walked around to the side, past the rose bushes that grew near the window. He could see the woman inside; no longer a girl, but all woman, Maria looked like someone who knew what she wanted and how to get it.

Handy Indian-toed it to the back door and tried the canvas covered outer door. It opened under his hand. It was warmer inside, and the air was close. There was a smell of food, and over it, of coffee.

He moved toward the lighted door and stopped as Maria framed herself there. Her breath caught, but she made no other sound. "Who are you?" she demanded. Maria, Handy saw, was not easily flustered.

"A driftin' cowhand who smelled fresh coffee and thought we might talk a little."

"We've nothing to talk about. Now rattle your hocks out of here before my man comes back."

"You mean Buck . . . or Salter?"

The beautiful eyes became less beautiful, but very cold and wary. "You'd better leave while you're able. If Buck should come back—"

"Maria," he said, "you're a beautiful woman. You're also a very smart one. By the time they've split that money so many ways there won't be enough left for your trouble. It won't hardly be enough for a woman like you."

"I don't know what you're talking about."

"Suppose only two of us was splitting it, and one of us wasn't greedy? I'm the kind of man who makes big money fast, so I'd not need half. I'd be happy with a third. Then I could ride on alone, or if you were so inclined—?"

There was cold calculation in her eyes now. Beautiful she might be, but Maria was dangerous as a rattler in the blind. Handy felt a little shiver go over him, and knew he could not relax for an instant when with this woman. Did Buck Rodd realize what dynamite he was playing with?

"How about that coffee, Maria?"

"I'll get it," she said.

She filled both cups and he watched, while seeming unconcerned.

"You're new around here." Her voice was low, almost friendly. He felt as a wild horse must feel at the soothing voice of a cowhand before he slipped the bit in his mouth.

"I've been new in a lot of places."

"Have I heard of you?"

"Wing Mathy thought he knew me."

"Then he will remember. Wing never forgets anybody, or anything."

"Maybe we won't be around then. That's a lot of money, Maria, and Frisco is a lot of town."

"What money are you talking about?"

"The money I got rooked out of. A few days ago over in Pagosa there was talk of a lot of cattle being sold. Damned poor prices, but these ranchers are all broke, anyway. I heard some talk, so I picked my spot and waited. The trouble was I waited too far up the road."

"What happened?" She was feeling him out now, trying him.

"How should I know? I didn't see it. However, I had heard about you and Salter. I also knew about you and Buck Rodd, which Salter didn't know. Fifteen thousand is a lot of money."

"You think I'd doublecross Buck Rodd for you?"

"Not for me, although the difference between what you'd get

from Buck and what you'd get from me might make me a lot
better looking."

Maria studied him. "If you were shaved you'd be quite a
handsome man. Fixed up, you'd look better than Buck Rodd."

"See what money does? I'm already looking better. Of course,
you don't need it. I never saw so much woman in one package
before. Finding somebody like you in a town like this makes
me believe in miracles."

"You'd need the miracle if Buck found you here. Or any of
his boys. They don't ask questions, believe me."

He smiled. "I know Buck Rodd."

"You don't seem buffaloed by him. Who are you, anyway?"

"Around here they call me Handy. In some other places they
called me Sonora Hack."

"Sonora Hack!" She caught her breath. "But you—you were
in prison!"

"Uh-huh. My horse stepped in a badger hole that time. They
got me. But as you can see, I'm not in prison now. I served my
time."

She was silent, refilling his cup. Obviously she was weighing
possibilities.

"Where's the money, Maria? Whatever we do has to be done
now. You tell me where that money is, and within a week we'll
be in Los Angeles on our way to Frisco."

"There's only one way you could do it. You'd have to kill
Buck Rodd, and the rest of them, too."

"That's quite a job."

He looked down into his cup. Not a half hour ago she had
been in Buck's arms; now she was telling him how to kill him.
Or was this a trap?

She put her hand over his. "Sonora! That's it! We could split
the reward, too! Nobody would guess that I have the money,
and if they were gone the case would be closed! They would
think the money was buried somewhere in the desert!"

"Where's the money, Maria? You tell me where it is and
give me that shotgun."

She laughed, her eyes dancing. She moved around the table
toward him. "Oh, no! You take the shotgun and do your part.

When you come back both the money and I will be waiting for you."

He swore inwardly. Of course, he had been sure that was the way she would be. He had no intention of using any kind of a gun unless it was forced on him. The money meant a lot to Bailey, to say nothing of the others, and he meant to get it back if he could. As for a piece of Bailey's ranch, that was a dream and no more than a dream. When Bailey discovered he was Sonora Hack he would have no further use for him. He certainly would not want him as a partner. Yet one thing he had established: Maria either had the money or knew where it was.

He looked down at her. "Maria, you don't think I'd trust you, do you? You an' me, we ride the same trail. We both want money, and a lot of it. You don't trust me, and I don't trust you, but if we work together we both stand to win."

"What do you want me to do?"

"Get the money now. Split in two halves. I'll take mine, and then you call Buck Rodd and tell him there's a man in your house. When he comes I'll be waiting."

He could almost feel her thoughts. How could she lose? If she stayed with them her part of the split would be a thousand dollars or less. Go his way and she could keep half, and she could find a way to get his half also.

If the worst happened, and Hack was killed, there was every chance Buck or some of his men would also be killed. Either way, her share would be larger.

Suddenly a new thought came to him. "What about Salter? Does he cut into this?"

She shrugged. "He was a fool! He agreed to run off with the money if somebody took care of Leeds. Wing Mathy and Carrero did that. When Salter got to where he was to meet me, Buck was waiting for him. It was a smooth job."

He stared at her from the shadows. Smooth, all right, and deadly, as ruthless and deadly as she herself.

"Good! Let's split the money now."

An instant she hesitated, then crossing the room she slipped back a portion of the base panel and got out a sack. "There it is, all of it."

A hinge creaked behind them and a cool young voice said, "I'll take that!"

Ann Bailey!

Sonora felt a shock of cold go through him. This was the end. Nobody would never believe he intended to get the money and return it.

She stepped into the room, her gun held steady. "Oh, you're contemptible! You promise to get our money back, and then you're here with this, this awful woman! You were planning to kill all those men! I heard it! I heard every word!"

Maria's eyes flashed at him. "I'll live to see you die, Sonora Hack!"

"Hack?" Ann's eyes flashed at him. "You?"

"That's right, and, although you'll never believe it, I intended to get that money back to you. I had first to find out where it was."

He could almost feel Maria's hatred. He saw Ann's left hand grasp the sack, saw her start backing toward the door. At that instant there was a heavy step on the front porch and a loud voice boomed out, "Maria? Where are you? The boys are comin' over!"

Ann stepped out the back door as the voice sounded, and in the startled instant of surprise at the voice, Maria grabbed for the shotgun.

Sonora hit the back door running; the shotgun bellowed, but he was outside and to the left, wheeling around the house with but one thought, to get out of range of the shotgun. Ann had vanished as if she were a ghost. He vaulted the front fence just as three men stepped down off the boardwalk in front of the saloon. His horse was a block away in the livery stable, saddled, fortunately.

Once he was on the buckskin . . . but Ann? What of Ann?

Behind him Rodd was shouting, and he saw the three outlaws start to run down the street toward him. He dove for an opening between two houses, heard a gun bark behind him, charged around the end of the house, and ran full-tilt into a woodpile and sprawled over it to the ground!

Scrambling to his feet, his hands stinging with pain from

the gravel, beyond the woodpile, he grabbed for his guns. He still had them.

A running man rounded a corner and he snapped a shot from the hip. It was a near miss, and the man yelped with surprise and fired in return. Sonora ducked into a crouch and ran, running from one building to another.

At least he was keeping them occupied, and he hoped Ann was getting away with the money. Where had she gotten to so quickly? And how had she gotten there in the first place? She must have followed him! Then she had never trusted him at all; but then, why should she?

His breath coming in racking gasps, he made the last building and rounded the corner. Behind him there was running and yelling. He flattened against the building at the corner. A man was standing in front of the livery stable, staring up the street to see what was happening.

A half-block up the street Gan Carrero, gun in hand, was surveying the street.

"Hsst!" Hack hissed.

The livery man turned his head sharply toward the sound. "Get that saddled buckskin out, pronto! Just turn him loose!"

The man ducked inside, and Sonora heard somebody blundering through the brush behind the building where he stood. Stepping into the street, he whistled shrilly for his horse.

Carrero wheeled and his gun came up, and Sonora fired. The outlaw stepped back. Sonora fired again, and Carrero fell to his face as the buckskin lunged from the stable, stirrups flopping.

Sonora hit the saddle on the fly, and the buckskin left town on a dead run. A bullet whistled by; another smacked viciously into some obstruction on his right. The buckskin was off and running now, and how that buckskin loved it!

Yet this was but the beginning; swinging into an opening under some cottonwoods, he began to circle back. What had become of Ann? They would want their money back, and they would want Ann dead, for she now knew of their guilt.

He walked the horse through the cottonwoods and up the slope toward a cut into the country beyond. The chaparral was thick, but there were plenty of openings, and he wove his way through. When he reached the cut he looked back. The lights of the town were plain, but he could see nothing else. Pursuit would be out there in the darkness, three deadly men and a woman, armed and prepared to kill.

Where was Ann? Scowling into the night, he tried to imagine what she would do, and how she would return to Pagosa. She knew the country much better than he for this was her home. Certainly, she would not keep to the trail, and if she had been shrewd enough to follow him she would be shrewd enough to think out an escape.

Yet behind her would be Buck Rodd, Shorty Hazel, and Wing Mathy. They would follow her, not him. She not only had the money, but her word could hang them.

Skirting a bluff, Hack rode down through a clump of Joshua trees where the cut was narrow. Due to the dip in the ground he would probably be unseen, so, dismounting, he knelt close to the earth and struck a match. He found no recent tracks.

Mounting, he started on through the cut. She should have a good start. His gunfight had delayed pursuit enough to give her a couple of miles start, which she could use to advantage. Her horse was probably a good one, and she would keep moving. Yet, her horse had been ridden the twenty miles from Pagosa, and perhaps the distance from her ranch to town.

Her pursuers would be on fresh horses, and would know the country as well as she.

The trail dipped and followed the bank of a small stream, which must be the same that flowed near Pagosa, and if so might offer an easy approach to the town. He again checked the trail for tracks.

Hoof prints! A horse had passed this way, perhaps within the last few minutes, for even as the match flared he saw a tiny bit of sand fall into one of the tracks.

A red-hot iron seemed to slash across his arm and, dropping the match, he dove off the trail, hearing a hard *spang* of a high-powered rifle.

He swung into the saddle, feeling the warm wetness of blood on his arm; yet he did not seem to have been badly hit, because his fingers were still working. Turning off the trail, he wove through the brush, keeping under cover. Pulling up for a

moment, he felt carefully with the fingers of his other hand.
The skin was only broken. With his bandana he made a crude
bandage to stop the flow of blood, which was slight in any case.

He was through in this country. Ann would escape now, and
would return to tell them what she had heard. She would also
tell them he was Sonora Hack, and they would discover he had
only recently been freed from prison. His chance of settling
down in Pagosa and making a place for himself would be
finished. Well, it had been a wild idea at best.

Remembering the conversation, he felt himself flushing to
think that she would believe he was that kind of man. That he
would plot with such a woman the cold-blooded murder of her
confederates.

In sullen despair he told himself to keep on riding. He was
finished here.

As if impelled by the thought, the buckskin started walking
up the long roll of the pinon-tufted mountainside, and Sonora
let him go. The buckskin quickened its pace and Hack, from
old habit, slid his gun from its holster and removed the shells
fired back at Hondo, then reloaded the pistol.

The buckskin, he realized, had found a trail, and now, of its
own volition, was traveling at an easy canter.

Buck Rodd would not give up easily. That was more money
than he was apt to see in a long time, and even if he had so
wished, Maria would not permit it. He would follow Ann back
to her ranch or to Pagosa.

Who in Pagosa could stand against him? Or the three together?

At this hour, there would be no one. Alerted, they might get
men together to greet them, but now there would be no time
for that. All three were men with notches on their guns, men
willing and ready to kill.

That was their problem. He had made his bid and messed
up. He should never have tried to get the money from Maria,
yet he had been so close!

Killing had been no part of his plan. He had hoped to get the
money back, leave Maria tied up, and return to Pagosa.

Remembering Ann's flashing eyes and vitriolic tongue, he
grinned despite himself. She was a terror, that one. The man
who got her would have his work cut out for him.

The thought of her belonging to some other man was a burr under the saddle-blanket of his thoughts. And he did not like to ride away leaving her with the opinion of him she now had. It would be an ugly picture.

With neither conscience nor the memories of a red-haired girl to afflict him, the buckskin cantered briskly along the trail, making good time. Hack rode along with the unconscious ease of a man long accustomed to the saddle, deep in his own thoughts. It was not until there was a sudden flash of light in the corner of his eyes that he came to with a start.

He was on the edge of Pagosa! The buckskin had very naturally headed for the stable where he had been taking it easy these past few days.

Realization hit him with a rush of horses' hoofs, and he saw three horsemen come charging up to a fourth. A girl screamed and a man opened the door of a house. A rifle shot rang out, and a harsh voice ordered, "Get back in there or I'll kill you! This is none of your affair!"

Another voice said, "Get the sack, Shorty."

"What about the girl? Do we take her along?"

"Hell, no! She'd be nothing but trouble. We'll find plenty of women below the border! We'll just leave her lay, to teach them a lesson!"

The buckskin felt the unexpected stab of the spurs and hit the trail running.

"Hey!" a voice yelled. "Look *out*!"

A gun roared almost in his face, a black body loomed before him, and he fired. A lance of flame leaped at him and he was in the midst of a wild tangle of plunging horses and shouting, swearing men. He caught a glimpse of Ann, hat gone, hair flying in the wind, breaking from the crowd and leaping her horse for the shelter of the buildings.

A head loomed near him and he slashed at it with his six-gun, seeing the man fall; then his horse swung around, and he was knocked from his horse but hit the ground staggering.

A big man rushed at him and he had just time to steady himself. He threw a hard punch into a corded belly, ripped up and uppercut, and then, from behind him as the man staggered, he heard somebody yell, "Look out, Rodd! Let me have him!"

Hack let go everything and hit the dirt just as a gun roared behind him.

Rodd grunted, gasped and then yelled. "You fool! You bloody fool! You've hit me! You've killed—!"

Shorty Hazel's voice shouted. "To Hell with it, Wing! Grab the bag and let's go!"

Hack rolled over and came to his knee shooting. Something hit him below the knee and he rolled over, coming up against the body of a man, who might be alive or dead. Something grated on gravel and the man lunged to his feet, sack in hand, and sprang for the nearest horse.

He steadied himself, leaning on one elbow, and fired. The man dropped the sack and turned.

Fire stabbed the darkness, and the body of the man beside him jerked slightly. Sonora Hack was holding his left hand gun and he fired in return. The other man turned, fell against his horse, then swung into the saddle.

Hack lifted his gun, then saw the sack lying in the road. "The Devil with it! Let him go!"

He tried to get to his feet, but one leg wouldn't function right. He crawled to the sack, felt the rustle of bills and the chink of gold coins. He got a grip on the sack and whistled.

The buckskin trotted to him and stood patiently while he caught hold of a stirrup and pulled himself up, then climbed into the saddle. He started the horse to the nearest house, gripping the sack in his right hand.

He shouted and the door opened, then other doors began to open, lamps were lighted, and people emerged. One of them was Ann. He thrust the sack at her. "Tryin' all the time. I was try—"

He felt himself falling, felt her hands catch him, then somebody else's hands. "He's passed out," somebody was saying. "He's—"

Something smelled like rain, rain and roses and coffee and other smells he could not place. Then he opened his eyes and he could hear the rain falling, and he stared out a curtained window at a pinon-clad hill beyond. Turning his head he saw his boots, wiped cleaner than they had been in months, and his gunbelt hanging near them, over the back of a chair. His clothes were folded neatly on the chair, and there was another chair, a rocking chair with a book lying face down on the seat.

The door opened and Ann Bailey came in. She was wearing an apron, and when her eyes met his, she smiled. "You're actually awake! You're not delirious!"

"What do you mean . . . delirious? Where am I? What's happened?"

"You're at home, on our ranch, and you were delirious. You talked," she blushed faintly, "an awful lot. You killed all those men."

"Not Rodd nor Hazel. Mathy killed Rodd by mistake. Hazel got away."

"He didn't get far. He fell off his horse about a mile down the road, and died before anyone found him."

"You got your money?"

"Of course." She looked down at him. "Half of this ranch is yours now."

"I won't take it. That isn't right."

"It is right. That was the deal, and we intend to stand by it. Anyway, Dad needs help. He's needed somebody who can handle cattle. He can't do it all himself. You get some rest now, and we can talk of that later."

"What's that I smell?"

"I'm making some doughnuts. Why?"

"All right. I'll stay. I always did like doughnuts!"

THE CARLISLE-KING FIGHT

When the wild towns of the Old West are listed it is always Abilene, Dodge City, Deadwood and Tombstone that are mentioned, and rarely Los Angeles.

Yet California in its early years was second only to Texas in the number of cattle roaming its thousands of hills, and the vaqueros who handled those cattle numbered among them some of the finest riders and ropers the country was to see.

The most noted gun battle of Los Angeles's early years took place on July 6, 1865, when Bob Carlisle shot it out with the King brothers at the old Bella Union Hotel.

On the afternoon of the previous day Carlisle had words with Under-Sheriff A. J. King over the investigation of the murder of John Rains, Carlisle's brother-in-law. The discussion ended with Carlisle using a Bowie knife on King, and during the argument he was supposed to have said that he could kill all the Kings.

Carlisle was a big, strikingly handsome man who had proved both his nerve and his skill with weapons on more than one occasion. As the son-in-law of Col. Isaac Williams and owner of the Chino Ranch of some 46,000 acres, he was a prominent citizen.

On the day following the difficulty between Carlisle and A. J. King, and just as the stage pulled up before the Bella Union, Frank and Houston King, brothers of A. J., were passing by and glimpsed Bob Carlisle through the open door.

Carlisle apparently saw them at the same time, and one of the Kings said, "There's Carlisle now. Let's go see if he means it."

As the King brothers approached the door, firing began. Carlisle's first bullet killed Frank King, but Houston King emptied his gun into Carlisle, putting four bullets within four inches of Carlisle's navel. Carlisle went down, then started to get up, and Houston rushed him, breaking his now empty pistol over Carlisle's head.

Pushing himself up against the wall, Carlisle gripped his six-shooter with both hands and shot Houston King through the body. Carried to a billiard table, Bob Carlisle died a short time later. Houston King survived the shooting and was tried for killing Carlisle, but acquitted.

Harris Newmark, a prominent citizen, came on the scene as the shooting ended, and has told the story in his memoirs, as has Frank King, former cowboy and writer who was the son of Houston King. There are several other accounts.

DOWN THE POGONIP TRAIL

It was cold, bitter, bitter cold, and the wind from off the mountains cut through even the warmest clothes. Jeff Kurland's clothes were not warm, for the long, dry summer had brought only disaster, and the few cattle he had been able to sell paid only for his groceries, leaving no margin for clothes.

Now he seemed to be facing another winter without snow, and it was melting snow which watered the grasslands far below, the grasslands where his cattle grazed. He bowed his head into the wind and headed his horse for the timber. Broke as a drunken miner after ten days in town, he would have no chance now of marrying Jill Bates.

The scarf tied around his head under his hat kept slipping down, but it did help to keep his forehead and the back of his neck warm. Without it, his brow would be cold as chilled iron, riding in this wind.

The mustang broke into a canter for the last few yards to the trees. They would be shelter from the wind, at least.

Now if he could just catch Ross Stiber! Five thousand dollars was a lot of money. Then he could fix up the cabin, get married, and maybe buy a few head of cattle to increase his small herd.

Only a few hours ago Sheriff Tilson had told him Stiber was believed to be hiding out somewhere in the icy peaks and ridges that loomed above Kurland's cabin. Tilson had warned him. The man was a killer.

139

If Tilson was smart, he would not go up into those peaks after Stiber. Jeff knew those peaks from harsh experience, and nothing could last a winter up there. All Tilson had to do was wait and watch. Stiber would have to come out.

The earth beneath his horse's hoofs was iron-hard, the sky above a dull, forbidding gray. Where the small creeks flowed, the rocks were sheathed with ice. On the trail that wound through the spruce he was at least out of the wind, and it was a mere three miles to his cabin.

Home! Four walls and a dirt floor, but a good fireplace and plenty of fuel. If a man was handy with an axe there was plenty of wood just from dead-falls, but food was scarce. What he would do if there were a heavy snowfall he could only guess.

Even his visit to Jill had turned out badly. Not that she was anything but adorable, or lacked affection, but the house was so warm and pleasant that he shuddered to think of her comments if she were to see his own harsh cabin.

He felt shy in the Bates's house. His clothes were shabby, and his big hands were blue with cold. He could hardly tear himself away from the fire for the warm meal, and when Kurt Saveth had started to banter him about his rugged life he had frozen up inside, unable to find words with which to reply. He was cold, resentful, and unhappy. It was no wonder Jill's parents preferred Saveth to him.

The worst of it was it was Saveth, from whom he bought supplies. It went against the grain to ask his rival for credit. Kurt knew how little he bought, how badly off he must be, and how things must be up there on his ranch.

The mustang's pace quickened. Cold as the barn might be, the horse was ready for it after the forty miles it had traveled this day. Jeff rode the gray into the yard and stepped down from the saddle. Leading the animal inside, he stripped off the gear, put a halter on him, and tied him to the manger. Then he forked down hay; at least he had plenty of that! He got out a blanket and covered the horse, buckling it in place. It was a light blanket, but at least it was some help against the cold. Fortunately, the barn was snug and secure from the raw wind. When Jeff Kurland built, he built well.

His steps were loud on the hard ground as he crossed the

frozen yard. Lifting the latch, he stepped inside and, dropping his sack of supplies, he started for the fireplace to light a fire.

He stopped short. Neatly piled atop the ashes was a small cone of twigs and shreds of bark.

"Don't make no sudden moves." The tone was harsh. "You just go ahead and light that fire. I was aimin' to do just that when you came into sight."

Without turning, Jeff struck a match and lighted the prepared fire. As it blazed up he added heavier sticks.

Of course, it would be Ross Stiber, and the man was a killer. Jeff half-turned his head. "All right to get up now? I'm not armed."

"Get up an' start fixin' some grub. Hope you brought somethin' with you. You surely ain't fixed for winter."

Jeff Kurland got up and glanced across the room at the man sitting on the bunk. He was a big, raw-boned man, unshaved, and with a heavy jaw. His bleak gray eyes were taking in Jeff Kurland, his worn clothes and thin face.

"I'm Stiber," he said, "but it ain't goin' to do you one particle of good."

He came up behind Jeff and ran a hand over his pockets. He sounded surprised when he stepped back. "No gun, huh? I already looked the cabin over, so where is it?"

"Ain't got one." Kurland was embarrassed.

"Don't get any ideas about that there *ree*ward. I'm wide awake all the time, and I can shoot the buttons off your coat."

"I know that. I just haven't got a gun."

Kurland went to work preparing the meal. He was hungry after his long ride, and wanted to eat. He also wanted time to think his way out of the situation he was in. How much of a situation, he was not sure. The outlaw settled himself back against the wall, watching his every move. Stiber seemed to want to talk.

"You sure aren't fixed well, friend. I looked your place over. Isn't enough grub here to feed a rat. How could you expect to last out a storm, no more grub than you've got?" He glanced at the sack Jeff had brought in. "An' you surely didn't pack much, considerin' you had a forty-mile ride."

Jeff was irritated, but he made no comment. What business

was it of Stiber's to come nosing around, butting into his business? If he was going without now and again, it was his business and nobody else's. He got coffee on and mixed biscuits.

"Shoulder of venison on the chair yonder," Stiber suggested. "Better fix it. I killed me a deer night before last. Not much game around. Must be the drouth." He glanced at Kurland. "Got your cattle, too, I'll bet."

He eased forward to the edge of the bunk again. "Hey? You got any smokin' in that bag? I run out of it up yonder in the peaks. I might have stuck it out if it hadn't been for that."

Jeff reached into the sack and tossed Stiber a package of tobacco. "Keep it," he said. "I've got another."

Stiber caught the sack and lowered it between his knees and got out some papers. "Thanks, amigo. Don't you just figure I'd have taken it, anyway? I could have. I probably would have, too. I wouldn't take both of them, though. A man can do without his grub, but his smokin'? No way.

"Up yonder in the peaks I smoked dried leaves; ain't done that since I was a youngster, shredded barl, just anything." He lit up and smoked in silence for several minutes. Then he said, "Who's the girl?"

Kurland's head came up sharply. He was as big as Stiber, but the hard months had made him lean. His eyes were bleak and dangerous. Stiber noticed it, and there was a flicker of humor in his eyes.

"Where's that picture? Did you take it?"

"What would I want with your picture? No, I didn't take it, an' I'm meanin' no disrespect. She's a right pretty girl, though."

"She's a fine girl and a decent girl."

"Did I say she wasn't?" Stiber protested. "Sure, she's a fine girl. I know her."

"*You* know her?" Jeff was startled.

"Jill Bates? I should smile, I know her. Don't look at me that way. Was a time when I wasn't no outlaw, havin' to hide out in the hills. I knew her when she was a youngster. Nine, ten years ago. I was a young cowpuncher then, drifted into this country after shootin' a man down at Santa Rita. That was my first shootin' and I was some upset. I wasn't fixin' to kill anybody. Then I met a girl up here. Blonde, she was. Cute as a bug's ear. Name of Clara Dawson."

Jeff grinned. "You should see her now."

"I don't aim to. Rather remember her as she was. Comes to that, I don't look so fine my own self. It was different then. About that time I was cuttin' a wide swath among the women-folks.

"You should have seen me then! Had me a silver-mounted saddle and bridle. Had a fine black horse, best one I ever owned. Comanches got him. I was lucky to get away with my hair."

"Come an' get it," Jeff put plates on the table. "You can put up that six-shooter, too. I don't plan on bustin' your skull until we've had something to eat."

Stiber chuckled. "Don't try it, boy. That's a right pretty little girl, and I'd hate to put tears in her eyes. Pour me some of that coffee, will you? Been two weeks since I've drunk coffee."

Stiber waited until the coffee was poured. He tucked the pistol in his waistband. "How come you haven't got a gun? I seen the holster."

Jeff flushed. "I borrowed money on it. From Kurt Saveth."

"Tough." Stiber was eating with obvious enjoyment. "You cook a mighty fine meal. You sure do." He looked up. "You fixin' to marry that Bates girl? If you are, you better go out and rob yourself a bank. You can't bring the likes of her to a place like this."

Jeff slammed down his fork. "Listen! You bust in here an' take a meal at gunpoint an' you can do it. I'd begrudge no man a meal! But you keep your nose out of my private business or I'll bust it all over your face!"

Stiber chuckled, lifting a protesting hand. "No offense! I was just talkin', that's all. As for bustin' my nose, even if I didn't have a gun you couldn't whip one side of me. Not that I'm aimin' to give you the chance.

"You fix a good meal, friend, but you make a wrong move and it will be the last one you ever fix. I've got five thousand in blood money restin' on my head, and that's a lot of money to a man in your fix."

Jeff ate in silence while the outlaw continued to talk. From time to time Jeff's thoughts returned to the subject of that reward. Five thousand dollars was a lot of money, and the man *was* wanted for a killing.

What was in Stiber's mind now? He scarcely dared try to leave the country, yet it was impossible to live among the peaks in this weather. It would be worse before it got better. Of course, if he had a good hideout—?

It was then Jeff Kurland remembered the cave on Copper Mountain.

Could that be where Stiber was hiding? Sheriff Tilson had said that Stiber did not know this country, yet if Stiber had been around here ten years ago, something Tilson obviously did not know, he might know of the cave on Copper Mountain.

Where else could a man live in those mountains in such cold? But had Stiber ever come through a *pogonip* fog in this country? Did he know what it was like when the fog turned to ice and settled in a chill blanket over everything?

If a man was caught in a cave, he'd better have plenty of food and be prepared to wait it out, because escape would be impossible. And unless Jeff Kurland was mistaken, the weather was shaping up for something like that now. Within the past few minutes he seemed to feel warmer, and not only because the room was heating up.

The outlaw's droning voice penetrated Jeff's thoughts.

"That Jill Bates, she's growed into a mighty handsome woman! Used to fetch her candy, I did, and maple sugar. That was when I was courtin' Clara. Thought the world of that kid. Even let her ride my black horse one time."

He pushed back his chair and got to his feet. "Got to be goin'. You split that grub in half, and leave me the sack. Ain't likely you'll have callers but I can't chance it."

"Listen," Jeff protested, "that's all the grub I've got! And I've no money!"

Ross Stiber chuckled. "You ain't sold your saddle yet, and I'll just bet that Kurt Saveth would like to buy it off you!"

"Sell my *saddle?* I'm not that broke! You know damned well that when a cowpuncher sells his saddle he's through . . . finished!"

"Then maybe you ain't quite finished. Why don't you go

slaughter one of Cal Harter's Pole Angus steers? I hear theirs
is the best beef you can find."

When he was gone Jeff dropped into a chair, thoroughly
discouraged. With the little grub he had brought in he *might*
have made it. As it was, he didn't have a chance.

Half the little food he had was gone, and he had no money
nor any chance to get any. Nor would anybody be hiring hands
in this kind of weather. They had let go what extra hands they
had for the winter season, keeping on just a few trusted stand-
bys. It looked like the end of everything. His chance to have
his own ranch, his chance to marry Jill, all gone down the
drain.

He had started his own outfit three years before, with three
hundred head of cattle. It was a herd carefully built from strays
or injured cattle. Here and there he bought a few head, mostly
calves from cattle drives, where the calves were an impedi-
ment. He had driven his herd into these high green valleys and
built his cabin.

In the months that followed he had labored to build a small
dam for a reservoir against the hot, dry months. Grass grew
well along the bottoms, and he had worked from daylight until
dark mowing hay with a scythe and stacking it against the long
winter ahead. He had built shelters of poles and brush, knowing the snow would bank against it and add to the warmth.
Nobody had held cattle up this high, but he believed he could
do it. A few years back he had come upon some wild cattle who
had survived a winter in the high country.

His first year had gone well. Although he lost a few head,
the calves more than made up for it, and during the summer
they increased and grew fat. Then had come a bitter winter
that shut down early, locking the land in an icy grip that broke
only in the late spring.

When he took stock he found he had lost over a hundred
head, and the others were gaunt and unfit for sale.

The summer had been hot and dry, and as it grew hotter and
dryer he had fought with all he had to keep his cattle in shape
and get them through until fall. Late rains, on which he had
depended, changed to snow, and now he was into the second
of the awful winters. Bigger cattlemen than he were hard hit,

but they had large herds and could stand some loss. Every one
he lost hurt severely. With all his money gone, he had sold off
his gear until all he had left was his Winchester .44 and his
riding gear.

Wearily, he got to his feet, banked the fire, and crawled into
his bunk, too exhausted to even worry.

He awakened to utter blackness and cold. Huddling in his
blankets, he dreaded the thought of the icy floor and the
shivering moments before he got the fire going.

The instant his feet hit the floor he felt an icy chill, and knew
at once what it was.

The *pogonip*! The dreaded fog that even the Indians feared,
an icy fog that put a blanket of death over every shrub, every
tree, even every blade of grass. Bitterly cold, and the ground
so slick it was inviting broken legs to even move, the air did
strange things with sound so that voices far away could be
distinctly heard.

Kicking back the blanket, he pulled on his socks and raced
across the floor to stir up the fire. Uncovering some coals, he
threw kindling into the fireplace and then raced back to the
warmth of his bed to wait until some of the chill had left the
cabin.

The kindling caught fire and the flames leaped up. After a
while he got out of bed, added more fuel, and put coffee water
on the fireplace stones. Then he dressed, and as he tugged on
his boots he saw the cigarette ashes spilled on the floor from
Stiber's cigarette.

Where was he now? Had he reached the cave on Copper
Mountain? Or had he realized what a trap it might be? The
cave was deep, and held a certain amount of warmth, but to
have reached it Stiber would have had to travel half the night
over rough and dangerous trails. Yet he might have done just
that.

On the third day of the *pogonip* snow fell, covering the ice
with a few scant inches of snow. Taking his rifle and slipping on
his snowshoes, he started his hunt. From now on life would be
a grim struggle to stay alive. He cruised through the woods,
seeking out likely places for deer. He had been out for more
than two hours and was slowly working his way back toward his

cabin when he saw a mule deer floundering in the deep snow. It was not until he killed it that he discovered its leg was already broken, evidently from a fall on the deadly ice.

The following day it snowed again, snowed slowly, steadily. Cold closed its icy fist upon the mountains, and his thermometer dropped to ten below, then to twenty below zero. On the morning of the tenth day it was nearly fifty below; his fuel supply was more than adequate, but it kept him adding fuel every fifteen to twenty minutes.

Long since, knowing the cold at this altitude, he had prepared for what was to come, stopping up all the chinks in the log walls, few though they were. He had squared off the logs with an adze when building the cabin, and they fit snugly. Only at the corners, carefully joined though they were, did some cold air get in. With newspapers he had papered the inside of the cabin, adding several layers of insulation.

With careful rationing of his venison, he figured he could get through the cold spell if it did not last too long.

Despite himself, he worried about the fugitive on Copper Mountain, if that was indeed where he was. Unless Stiber had been able to kill some game, he would by this time be in an even worse situation than himself. And in this kind of weather there would be no game in the high country.

Awakening a few days later, Jeff Kurland lay in bed, hands clasped behind his head. The thought of Stiber alone on Copper Mountain would not leave him. Outlaw and killer he might be, but it was not Jeff's way to let even an animal suffer. If Ross Stiber had been in the cave on Copper Mountain he would surely have come out by now, and there was no other way out except right by this cabin.

He made his decision suddenly, yet when he thought of it he knew the idea had been in his mind for days. He was going to scale Copper Mountain and find out just what had happened to Stiber. The man might have broken a leg and be starving in his cave.

The air was crisp and still, colder than it seemed at first. Buckling on his snowshoes and slinging his rifle over his shoulder, Jeff Kurland hit the trail. Knowing the danger of perspiring in this cold, he kept his pace down, despite his anxiety.

Sweat-soaked undergarments could quickly turn to a sheath of ice in such intense cold. After that, freezing to death was only a matter of time.

The trail wound upward through a beautiful forest of lodge-pole pine which slowly gave way to scattered spruce as he climbed higher on the mountain. Despite the slow pace he made good time, and would reach the most difficult stretch shortly before noon. Deliberately, he refused to think about the return trip.

Pausing once, on a flat stretch of trail, he looked up at the mountain. "Kurland," he told himself, "you're a fool."

What he was doing made no kind of good sense. Ross Stiber had chosen the outlaw trail, and if it ended in a cave on Copper Mountain instead of a noose it was only what he might have expected. It might even be what Stiber would prefer.

Jeff knew the route, although he had visited the cave but twice before. After reaching the shelf there would be no good trail, and his snowshoes offered the only way of getting there at all.

The air was death still, and the cold bit viciously at any exposed flesh. He plodded on, taking his time. Fortunately, on this day there was no wind. His breath crackled, freezing as he breathed. He walked with extreme care, knowing that beneath the snow there was ice, smooth, slick ice.

When he reached the stretch of trail along the face of Red Cliff, he hesitated. The snow was very thin along that trail where the wind had blown, and beneath it was the slick ice of the *pogonip*. The slightest misstep and he would go shooting off into space, to fall on the ice-covered boulders four hundred feet below.

On this day he was wearing knee-high moccasins with thick woollen socks inside. They were better for climbing, and worked better with the snowshoes.

Removing the snowshoes, he slung them over his back and, keeping his eyes on the trail a few feet ahead, he began to work his way along the face of the cliff.

Once fairly on his way there was no turning back, for turning around on the slick trail, while it could be done, was infinitely more dangerous than continuing on. It took an hour of painstaking effort to traverse the half-mile of trail, but at last, panting and scared, he made it. Ahead of him towered the snow-covered bulk of what was locally called Copper Mountain.

He scanned the snow before him. No tracks. Not even a rabbit had passed this way. If Ross Stiber was actually living on the mountain, he had not tried to come this way.

Carefully, he worked his way up along the side of the mountain, keeping an eye out for Stiber. The man might see him, shoot, and ask questions later. If there were anything left alive to question.

White and silent, the mountain towered above the trees, and Jeff paused from time to time to study it, warily, for fear of avalanches. Under much of that white beauty there was *pogonip* ice, huge masses of snow poised on a surface slicker than glass, ready to go at any instant. He put his snowshoes on once more and started, very carefully, along a shoulder of the mountain.

Only a little way further now. He paused, sniffing the air for smoke. There was none. Nor was there any sound.

The mouth of the cave yawned suddenly, almost unexpectedly, for with snow covering the usual landmarks he had no longer been sure of its position. The snow outside the cave was unbroken. There were no tracks, no evidence of occupation.

Had he come all this way for nothing?

He ducked his head and stepped into the cave. Unfastening his snowshoes, he left them at the entrance and tiptoed back into the cave. Lighting a branch of fir for a torch, he held it high to get the most from its momentary light. It was then he saw Stiber.

The outlaw lay upon a bed of boughs covered with some blankets and his coat. Nearby were the ashes of a fire, long grown cold. Here, away from the mouth, the cold was not severe, but, taking one glance at Stiber's thin, emaciated face, Jeff Kurland dropped to his knees and began to kindle a fire.

He got the fire lighted using half-burned twigs and bits of bark, then he hurried outside the cave for more fuel. All that in the cave had evidently been burned long since.

As the flames leaped up and the cave lightened, Stiber's

eyes opened and he looked at Kurland. "You, is it? How did you get here?"

"The same way you did. Over the trail from my place. I was worried."

"You're a fool, if you worried about me. I ain't worth it, and you've no call to worry."

"I was afraid you'd busted a leg."

"You guessed right," Stiber said, bitterly. "My leg is busted. Right outside the cave, on the first morning of that ice fog. I dragged myself back in here and got some splints on it."

"How's your grub?"

"Grub? I run out seven days ago."

Jeff opened his pack and got out some black tea. He was a coffee man, himself, but he carried the tea for emergencies, and now he brewed it hot and strong.

"Try this," he said when it was ready, "and take it easy. The cup's hot."

With water from his canteen and some dried venison he made a broth, thickening it a little with corn flour.

Stiber put his cup down and eased himself to a sitting position. "Figured tea was a tenderfoot drink," he said, "but it surely hits the spot."

"Best thing in the world if you're in shock or rundown. Wait until you get some of this broth."

Later, a flush on his cheeks and warmed by the hot drinks and the fire, Ross Stiber looked over at Kurland with cold gray eyes. "Well, this is your show. You're here, and the grub you brought won't last more than two days. What d' you figure to do?"

Kurland had been thinking of that. In fact, he had been thinking of it all the way up, and there was only one possible answer.

"Come daybreak I'm packing you out of here."

"You've got to be crazy. You couldn't pack a baby over that icy trail! And I'm a full-grown man."

"Get some sleep," Kurland said, "and shut up before I change my mind and leave you here."

At daybreak he was up. Deliberately, he kept his thoughts away from the ordeal before him. It was something he had to do, no matter how much he feared it, no matter how much he disliked the injured man.

He helped Stiber into all the clothes he had, then wrapped him in a heavy blanket. "You will be heavy, but you'll not be moving, and I don't want you frozen. You will be just that harder to carry."

With a stick, Stiber hobbled to the cave mouth. The morning was utterly still and bitterly cold. "You'll never make it. Go down alone and send them after me."

"They wouldn't come. Nobody but a damn' fool would tackle that trail before spring, and I'm the damn fool."

He studied the trail for a moment, calculating. It did no good to look. He already knew how tough it was, and what he had to do.

"Once I get you on my back," he said, "don't move. Don't talk, don't even wiggle a toe."

When he had his snowshoes adjusted, he took the injured man on his back and started over the snow. The man was heavy, and there was no easy way to carry him. "You'll have to hang on," he said. "I'll need my hands."

Step by careful step, he worked his way over the snow toward the head of the eyebrow trail along the cliff face. At the near end of that trail he lowered the injured man to the snow.

Leaving Stiber on the snow he slung his snowshoes over his back and went out on the narrow thread of trail. The very thought of attempting to carry a man over that trail on his back sent cold prickles of fear along his spine. Yet there was no other way.

Now, scouting the trail with care, he tried to envision every step, just how he would put his feet down, where there was the greatest danger of slipping, where he could reach for a handhold.

Reaching the end of the trail, he left the snowshoes and rifle, then returned for Stiber. Resolutely, he refused to accept the obvious impossibility of what he intended to do. The man would die if he did not get him out. That he might die in the attempt was not only possible, it was likely. Yet he had spent years in the mountains, and he knew his strength and his skill.

He had to depend on that. Was he good enough? That was the question.

When he returned he sat down beside Stiber. The outlaw looked at him quizzically. "I wasn't really expectin' you back."

"You're a liar. You knew damned well I'd be back. I'm just that kind of a damned fool."

"What happens now?"

"I'm packing you, piggyback, over that trail."

"Can't be done. There's no way it can be done. Man, I weigh two hundred and twenty pounds."

"Maybe two weeks ago you weighed that. I'd lay fifty bucks that you don't weigh over two hundred right now."

Using a nearby tree Stiber pulled himself erect and Kurland backed up to him. Careful not to injure the broken leg Kurland took the man on his back. "Now, whatever you do, don't even wiggle. You can throw me off balance on that trail. If you do, we're both gone."

He avoided looking at the trail now. He knew very well what faced him and that he must take the trip one step at a time. The slightest misstep and both would go over the brink. Under the snow was the ice of the *pogonip*.

Carefully, he put a foot out, testing for a solid foothold. Wearing moccasins, he could feel the unevenness, even grip a little with his toes. Little by little, he edged out on the trail. Icy wind plucked at his garments and took his breath. He did not look ahead, feeling for each new foothold before he put his weight down.

Sweat broke out on his face, trickled down beside his nose. Desperately, he wanted to wipe it away but there was no chance, for his arms were locked under Stiber's knees.

How long a trail was it? A half-mile? He could not remember. His muscles ached. Dearly, he wanted to let go just a little, to rest even for a moment. Once, just past the middle, his foot slipped on the icy trail, and for an instant their lives hung in the balance. Jeff felt himself going, but Stiber's knees gripped him tighter.

"Get your feet under you, lad." Stiber's voice was calm. "I've got hold of a root."

Darkness was falling when at last they came to the cabin. Over the last miles Kurland had dragged Stiber on a crude travois made of branches, holding the ends of two limbs in his hands while dragging Stiber over the snow, lying on his make-shift litter. When they reached the cabin, he picked the big man up and carried him inside, and dumped him on the bunk.

The cabin was icy inside, and hurriedly Jeff Kurland built his fire. Soon there was a good blaze going, and warmth began to fill the room. An hour later, Stiber looked at him over a bowl of hot soup.

"Now you can turn me in for that *ree*ward," he said, almost cheerfully.

Kurland's head snapped up. He felt as though he had been slapped.

"Go to blazes! I didn't risk my neck getting you down off that mountain just to see you hung. When you can walk, you get out of here, and stay out!"

"No need to get your back up. I wouldn't blame you. I et up half your grub, and caused you no end of grief."

Jeff Kurland did not reply. He knew only too well the long, difficult months that lay ahead, and that when spring came there would be hardly enough cattle left to pay off his debts, if there were any at all. He would have nothing with which to start over.

Moreover, if he did not report Ross Stiber, and if he was caught with the man in his cabin, he could be accused of harboring a criminal. The fact that the man had a broken leg would help him none at all.

At the same time, he knew he could not turn him in. One cannot save a man's life without having a certain liking for him thereafter, nor can a man share food with another without developing a feeling of kinship, for better or worse.

He did not want Stiber in his cabin. He resented the man. His food was all too limited, and game was scarce. Nor did he like Stiber's company, for the man talked too much. Yet he could not turn him in. He would wait until the leg was mended, when Stiber would have a running chance, at least.

The cold held the land in a relentless grip. More and more

snow fell. Finally, desperate for food, he killed one of his steers. The fuel supply burned low, and Kurland fought his way through the snow to the edge of the timber, where he felled several trees and bucked them up for fuel. Stiber watched, with small gray eyes holding a flicker of ironic humor.

"You live through this winter an' you'll have a story to tell your grandchildren."

Kurland glared. "What grandchildren? What chance would I have to marry Jill with a setup like this?" He waved a hand at the earthen floor and the shabby bunk. "I was hoping for some good years. I was planning to build a cabin up yonder, where there's a view, close to the spring. It would have been a place for any woman."

"You should have kept your gun. You could have stuck up the Charleston stage. She carries a sight of money sometimes."

"I'm no thief! You tried it, and where did you wind up? Half-frozen in a cave on Copper Mountain!"

"That's no more than plain truth," he admitted. "Well, each to his own way. I took mine because I killed a man. He wasn't much account, either. I end up starvin' in a cave, and you starve in this miserable cabin. Neither of us gets much of a break."

"I'll make my own breaks," Kurland replied. "Just wait until spring. I'll get me a riding job and save some money."

Stiber's tone was mocking. "At forty a month how much are you goin' to save? You think that girl will wait? Maybe somebody else is shinin' up to her? Somebody who doesn't freeze and starve on hopes? You think she'll wait? A time comes for marriage, and a woman marries, doin' the best she can. You're dreamin', boy."

Maybe he was. Jeff Kurland stared into the fire. He had been taking too much for granted. What made him think she loved him? Because he loved her? Because he wanted her love so much?

He had never so much as spoken of his dreams to her, just the simple facts of the case, yet how many times must she have heard that? Every cattleman, sheepman, and mining man had the same dream. And all the while there was Kurt Saveth, who had a small but charming home in town which he had inherited from his folks; he also had a successful store, and people around all the while, not a lonely cabin in the far-up mountains.

Footsteps crunching in the snow caused his head to lift. Ross Stiber's grab for his pistol was just an instant slower than Jeff's. "Not today, Stiber! We will have no shooting here!"

There was a loud knock, and at his "Come in!" the door opened and Sheriff Tilson entered, followed by Kurt Saveth, looking handsome in a new mackinaw, and following him, Doc Bates, and, of all people, Jill!

His face flushed with shame. He had not wanted her to see how he lived until he had something better, something fit to show her. He saw her glance quickly around, but as her eyes came to him he looked quickly away.

"All right, Stiber, you're under arrest." He turned to Jeff. "What's this mean, Kurland? You harborin' this outlaw?"

"He has a broken leg," Jeff spoke with dignity. "What could I do, carry him down on my back?"

"You could report it," Tilson replied. "You're in trouble, young man."

"He found me dyin' in the cave on Copper Mountain, Sheriff. He packed me over Red Cliff trail on his back."

"You expect me to believe that? After that *pogonip* a rabbit couldn't come down that trail, to say nothing of a man packin' another man on his back."

"He done it," Stiber insisted. "I'd come down and taken grub away from him, but when he figured I was starving he came up and got me. I'm his prisoner. If there is any reward he should get it."

Tilson laughed with humor. He glanced around at Saveth. "Hear that? They'd probably split it. Your guess that Stiber was hidin' here was a good one, Kurt. He had to be here, because there's no other place on the mountain where he could keep warm."

Doc Bates looked around from examining Stiber's leg. "This man does have a broken leg, Tilson."

"That doesn't make Kurland's story true. No man in his right mind would risk that trail. Kurland will be lucky if we don't prosecute him."

Jeff Kurland felt nothing but disgust and despair. He did not care about the reward. He had never thought seriously of that, anyway, but he sensed that Saveth disliked him and wanted him out of the way. Well, this ended it. When the cold broke he'd sell whatever he had left and head south.

Then he felt a hand slip into his. Startled, he looked down to see Jill had moved close beside him.

She was looking at Ross Stiber. "I remember you. You're Jack Ross, the rider from Cheyenne."

"You've a good memory, ma'am. Look, don't you believe what they're saying. All they want is that reward money. You've got your hand on the best and squarest man I know. If you take your hand off his arm you'll have lost the best of the breed."

"We'll fix a travois and haul him down to jail," Tilson said, and he glanced at Jeff. "You'll have a tough time provin' you didn't harbor a criminal."

"Sheriff," Doc Bates interrupted, "I know this man Stiber. He may be wanted as an outlaw, but I can put fifty men on the stand that will testify he's no liar. Before he got into trouble Jack Ross, that's how we knew him, was a respected man and a top hand. If he says Kurland brought him over the Red Cliff trail, I'll believe him. So will those others."

"And I'll swear to it on the stand," Stiber added. "He had me. I was his prisoner."

"We'll see about that," Saveth said.

Tilson was irritated. "Let's get out of here," he said. "Doc? You comin' with us?"

"I guess we all are," Bates said. "We wouldn't want anything to happen to our prisoner now, would we?"

Tilson went outside to put together a travois, and Stiber turned quickly to Jill. "Ma'am? You won't be tellin' Clara that I'm Jack Ross now, will you? I wouldn't want her to see me in jail. Not that she meant much to me. Fact is, I was glad to get away. She struck me as one of those who'd get mean and cantankerous as she grew older."

"You were right about that," Jeff assured him. "She has a disposition like a sore-backed mule. Just ask Tilson."

"Does he know her?"

"*Know* her? He married her!"

All the way to town Sheriff Tilson wondered if Ross Stiber wasn't a little crazy. He kept chuckling and laughing, and what did a man with a broken leg, maybe headed for a hanging, what did he have to laugh about?

GABRIEL VS. PHY

There were only a few occasions when top gunfighters shot it out with each other. One of these was the meeting of Pete Gabriel and Joe Phy.

The two had known each other for some time, and had been friendly until they campaigned against one another for sheriff. Pete won the election, but during the campaign tales had been carried back and forth by those interested in creating trouble. Bad blood developed as a result, and there was considerable speculation as to what would happen when and if they fought.

Joe Phy was a professional gambler and a gentleman. He dressed with care, conducting himself with reserve and dignity. He neither smoked nor drank, but was widely known for his skill with guns.

When the showdown came it was in a saloon in Florence, Arizona. Phy was the faster of the two, and there was no question as to his accuracy. He emptied his pistol, putting all five bullets into Gabriel's body, one of them close to his heart.

Pete Gabriel, a tough man and a good law officer, fired but one shot, killing Phy. Gabriel survived the fight and lived for a number of years.

WHAT GOLD DOES
TO A MAN

We came up the draw from the south in the spring of '54, and Josh was the one who wanted to stop.

Nothing about that country looked good to me, but I was not the one who was calling the shots. Don't get the idea that it was not pretty country, because it surely was. There was a-plenty of water, grass, and trees. That spring offered some of the coldest and best water I ever tasted, but I didn't like the look of the country around. There was just too much Indian sign.

"Forget it, Pike!" Josh Boone said irritably. "For a kid, you sound more like an old woman all the time! Believe me, I know gold country, and this is it. Why should a man go all the way to California when there's gold all around him?"

"It may be here," Kinyon grumbled, "but maybe Pike Downey ain't so dumb, even if he is a kid. He's dead right about that Injun sign. If we stick around here, there being no more than the five of us, we're apt to get our hair lifted."

Kinyon was the only one who thought as I did. The others had gold fever, and had it bad, but Kinyon's opinions didn't make me feel any better, because he knew more about Injuns than any of the rest. I'd rather have been wrong and safe.

Josh Boone did know gold country. He had been in California when the first strike was made, and I don't mean the one at

161

Sutter's Mill that started all the fuss. I mean the *first* strike, which was down in a canyon near Los Angeles. Josh had done all right down there, and then when the big strikes came up north he'd cleaned up some forty thousand dollars, then he rode back east and had himself a time. "Why keep it?" he laughed. "There's more where that came from!"

Maybe there was, but if I made myself a packet like that I planned to buy myself a farm and settle down. I even had the place in mind.

It was Boone who suggested we ride north away from the trail. "There's mountains yonder," he said, "and I've a mind there's gold. Why ride all the way to Californy when we might find it right here?"

Me, I was ready. Nobody would ever say Pike Downey was slow to look at new country. The horse I rode was the best in the country, and it could walk faster than most horses could trot. It weighed about fourteen hundred, and most of it muscle. It was all horse, that black was, so when we turned off to the hills I wasn't worried. That came later.

Josh Boone was our leader, much as we had one. Then there was Jim Kinyon, German Kreuger and Ed Karpe. I was the kid of the bunch, just turned nineteen, strong as a young bull.

Josh had been against me coming along, but Kinyon spoke for me. "He's the best shot I ever did see," he told them, "and he could track a snake upstream in muddy water. That boy will do to take along."

Kinyon calling me a boy kind of grated. I'd been man enough to hold my own and do my part since I was fourteen. My paw and maw had come west from Virginia in a covered wagon, and I was born in that wagon.

I'd been hunting since I was knee-high to a short beaver, and the first time I drove a wagon over the Santa Fe Trail I was just past fourteen. My rifle drew blood for me in a Comanche attack on that wagon train, and we had three more fights before we came up to Santa Fe.

Santa Fe was wild and rough, and I had a mix-up with a Comanchero in Santa Fe with knives, and I put him down to stay. The following year I went over the Trail again, and then I went to hunting buffalo in Texas. The year after I went all the way to California, and returning from that trip I got friendly with some Cheyennes and spent most of a year with them, raiding deep into Mexico. By the time I met Boone, I had five years of the roughest kind of living behind me.

Boone talked himself mighty big, but he wasn't bigger than me, and neither was Ed Karpe.

We rode up that draw and found ourselves the prettiest little canyon you'll ever see, and we camped there among the trees. We killed us a deer, and right away Josh went to panning that stream. He found gold from the first pan.

Gold! It ran heavy from the first pan, and after that there was no talking to them. We all got to work, but being a loner I went along upstream by myself. Panning for gold was something I had never done, but all the way back from California that time I'd traveled with one of the best, and he'd filled me to the ears with what was needful to know about placer mining for gold.

He told me about trying sandbars and little beaches where the stream curves around and throws up sand in the crook of the elbow. Well, I found such a place, and she showed color.

Wasting no more time on panning, I got my shovel and started digging down to bedrock. No more than four feet down I struck it. It was cracked here and there and, remembering what that old timer told me, I cleaned those cracks and went back under the thin layers of rock and panned out what I found. By nightfall I had a rawhide sack with maybe three or four hundred dollars in it.

All of the boys had gold, but none of them had as much as I showed them, which was less than half what I had. Jim Kinyon was tickled, but it didn't set too well with either Boone or Karpe. Neither of them liked to be bested, and in particular they didn't like it from me.

Kreuger patted me on the back. "Goot poy!" he said. "Das iss goot!"

We took turns hunting meat, and next day it fell to me. Mounting up, I took my Sharps Breech-Loader, and I'd buckled on my spare pistol. I had me two Army Colts, Model 1848, and I set store by them guns. I'd picked 'em off a dead Texan down east of Santa Fe.

That Texas man had run up on some horse thieves and out of luck at the same time. There'd been four horse thieves and him, and they had at it, and when I came along some hours later there they lay, all good dead men with a horse for each and six extry. There were their rifles, pistols, and a good bit of grub, and there was no sense in leaving it for the Comanches to pick up or the sand to bury. In the time I'd been packing those six-shooters I'd become right handy with 'em.

They were riding my belt that morning when I rode out from camp. Sighting a couple of deer close to camp, I rode around them. I'd no mind to do my killing close by, where we might need the game at some later time. A few miles further away I fetched me a good-sized buck, skinned him out, and cut us some meat. Down at the stream I was washing the blood from my hands when I glanced up to see two things at once—only one of them was important at the moment.

The first thing I spotted was a full-growed Injun with his bow all drawn back and an arrow aimed at me. Throwing myself to one side I fetched one of those Colts and triggered me an Injun just as the arrow flicked past my face. He slid down off that river bank and right into the Happy Hunting Grounds, where no doubt someday we'll meet and swap yarns.

The other thing I'd glimpsed was upstream just a ways. It was only a glimpse, but I edged along the creek for a better look.

Under a ledge of rock, just above the water, was a hole. It was about crawling-into size, and didn't smell of animal, so I crawled in and stood up. It was a big cave, a room maybe twenty feet long by fifteen wide, with a solid-packed sandy floor and a smidgin of light from above. Looking up, I could see a tangle of branches over a hole, which was a couple of feet across but well-hidden by brush.

When I rode into camp to unload my meat I told the boys about my Injun. "I caved the bank over him," I said, "but they will most likely find him. Then they'll come hunting us."

"One more and one less," Karpe said. "A dead Injun is a good Injun."

"A dead Injun is the start of trouble," I said. "We'd better light out of here if we want to keep our hair."

"Are you crazy?" Boone stared at me. "With all the gold we're finding?"

"We don't need to leave the country," I protested. "But what does gold mean to a dead man?"

"The boy is right," Kinyon agreed. "We're in for trouble."

"We can handle trouble," Karpe said. "I ain't afeerd of no Injuns. Anyway, this just sounds like Pike talking big. I'll bet he never saw no Injun."

Well, I put down the meat I was eating and licked my fingers. Then I got up and looked across the fire at him. "You called me a liar, Ed," I said, mild-like. "I take that from no man."

He stared at me like he couldn't believe what he was hearing. "Now what about this?" he said. "The boy figures he's a growed-up man! Well, I'll take that out of him!" He got to his feet.

"No guns," Boone said. "If there are Injuns, we don't want to draw them nigh."

Me, I shucked my Bowie. Some folks don't fancy cold steel, and Ed Karpe seemed to be one of them. "Shuck your steel, Ed," I told him. "I'll see the color of your insides."

"No knives," he protested. "I fight with my hands or a gun."

I flipped my knife hard into a log. "All right," I said. "It makes me no mind. You just come on, and we'll see who is the boy of this outfit."

He come at me. Ed Karpe was a big man, all rawboned and iron hard. He fetched me a clout on the jaw that made me see lights flashing, hitting me so hard I nearly staggered. Then he swung his other fist but I stepped inside, grabbing him by shirt-front and crotch, swinging him aloft and heaving him against the bank.

He hit hard, but he was game and came up swinging. He fetched me a blow, but he was scared of me grabbing him and hit me whilst going away. I made as if to step on a loose rock and stagger, and he leapt at me. Dropping to one knee, I caught him again by shirt-front and crotch, only this time I throwed him head first into that bank. He hit hard and he just laid there.

When I saw he wasn't about to get up, I dusted off my knees

and went back to the bone I'd been picking. Nobody said anything, but Josh Boone was looking surprised and sizing me up like he hadn't really seen me before. "You can fight some," he admitted. "That didn't take you no time at all."

"One time up in Pierre's Hole I fought nigh onto two hours with a big trapper. He'd have made two of Ed there, and he was skookum man, but I whopped him some."

After a bit Ed Karpe come around, and he come back to the fire shaking his head and blinking, but nobody paid him no mind. Me, I was right sorry. It ain't good for folks to start fighting amongst themselves in Injun country. Come daylight I went back to my shaft and taken one look. Whilst I'd been grub-hunting yesterday somebody had moved in and cleaned the bed-rock slick as a piano-top.

Sure, I was upset, but I said nothing at all right then. I went on up the creek to a better place and dug me another hole, only when I left this one I covered it with brush and wiped out the sign I'd left.

Kinyon had been hunting that day, and when he came in he was worried. "We'd better light out or get fixed for a fight. There's Injuns all around us."

They listened to Kinyon where they hadn't listened to me, so we dug ourselves some rifle pits and forted up with logs. I said nothing about my shaft being cleaned out.

Next day I went back to my brush-covered hole and sank her down to bedrock and cleaned up. This was heavy with gold, and the best so far. My method of going to the rock was paying off. It was more work than using a pan, and it was more dangerous.

That night when we all came in to camp Kreuger was missing. We looked at one another, and believe me, we didn't feel good about it. Nobody had seen the German, and nobody had heard a shot. When morning came I headed upstream, then doubled back to where Kinyon was working, only I stayed back in the brush. I laid right down in the brush not far from him, but where I could watch both banks at once.

"Jim?" I kept my voice so only he would hear me. "Don't you look up or act different. I'll do the talking."

"All right," he said.

"Somebody robbed that shaft of mine. Cleaned her out whilst I was hunting."

He wiped sweat from his face but said nothing.

"I've some ideas about German Kreuger, too."

"You think he stole your gold and lit out?"

"You know better. Nor do I think Injuns killed him. However, we better have us a look."

"Who do you think?"

"It wasn't you, and it wasn't me. And I'd bet every ounce I have that it wasn't that old German."

Pausing, I said, "You go on working. I'll watch."

He was canny, Jim was. He worked, all right, but he didn't get into a pattern. When he bent down he didn't lift up in the same place, but away from there. He kept from any pattern, so's if anybody planned a shot they'd have to wait until he was out in the open.

As for me, I almost missed it. Almost, but not quite. I'd been lying there a couple of hours, and my eyes were tired. The day was warm, and I'd been working hard the past few days and was tuckered. I must have been looking right at that rifle barrel a full minute before I realized it.

Only the fact that Kinyon was moving saved him. He was down by the water, partly hidden by some rocks, and he was digging sand from the low side of a boulder, preparing to wash it out. That rifleman was waiting for him to come up on the bank where he'd have no doubt.

Me, I didn't wait. Sliding my old Sharps breechloader up, I just threw a shot into that brush, right along that rifle barrel. There was a crash in the brush, and both me and Jim jumped for it, but the heavy brush and boulders got in the way, and by the time we got there that feller was gone. Nor could we make anything from the tracks except that he wore boots and was therefore a white man.

We tried to track him, though, and found nothing until we slid down among some rocks and there we found Kreuger. He'd been scalped. "No Injun," Kinyon said, and he was right. That was plain as day to any old Injun fighter.

"We've got a murderer in the outfit," I said.

"Maybe," Kinyon said doubtfully, "but there could be somebody else around, somebody we don't know about."

After a pause he said, "We've not much gold yet."

"No one of us has," I agreed, "but for one man it's a healthy stake, if he had it all."

"Injuns around," Kinyon said, that night at the fire. "Today I was shot at."

"I've been afraid of that," Karpe agreed. "We'd better watch ourselves."

Josh Boone glanced over at Karpe. "It ain't Injuns that scares me," he said, but if Ed Karpe noticed he paid no attention.

For the next two days everything went along fine. I worked with an eye out for trouble, and every now and again I'd quit work and scout around the area to make sure nobody was closing in on me. On the bottom of the shaft I'd sunk, I broke up the layers of bedrock where there were cracks, and made a good cleanup. Even me, who'd been doing well, couldn't believe how rich the find was. When I sacked up that night I had more than I'd had in my life, more than I'd ever seen, in fact.

Kinyon met me at an agreed-upon place on the creek bank. "Let's go higher," I suggested, "and sink a shaft together. We'll work faster, and this ground is rich enough for both of us."

Ed Karpe came up to us. He looked from one to the other. "I'd like to throw in with you boys," he said. "I'm getting spooked. I don't like going it alone." He looked at us, his face flushing. "Maybe I've lost my nerve."

"Why do you say that?" I asked.

"I feel like somebody's scouting me all the time."

Boone joined us just then, carrying his rifle in the hollow of his arm. "What's this? Everybody quitting so soon?"

"We're going to team up and work together," I said. "We figure it will be safer. Less chance of Injuns sneakin' up on us. I think we should get what we can and move out while our luck holds."

Josh Boone stared at me. "You runnin' this show now? I thought I was elected leader?"

"You was," Kinyon agreed. "It wasn't any idea of leading that started Pike talking. He figures we'd all do a lot better working together on shares than each working by himself."

"Oh, he does, does he? I don't see he's done so durned well."

"I got more than four thousand in gold. If any of you has over a thousand I'll cook chow this night."

"*Four thousand?*" They just stared. Jim was the one who said it, then he spat into the dust. "What're we waitin' for? I ain't got five hundred."

That settled it, but it did not settle Josh Boone. He was sore because they all listened to me now. Even Karpe listened, although I was keeping an eye on Karpe. He kept his gun close and his eyes busy, but mostly he was watching me. I saw that right off.

We were edgy, all of us. Here we were, four men out miles from anywhere or anybody, hid out in the Black Hills, but we watched each other more than we watched for Injuns.

German Kreuger was gone, so our little world was lessened by one, our total strength less by twenty percent, our loneliness increased by the missing of a face by the fire at night.

Somebody, either Karpe, Boone, or some stranger had killed Kreuger, and had been about to shoot Jim Kinyon. Only we had found no stranger's tracks, nor even the tracks of any Indian at the time.

Our meat gave out, and Karpe was the hunter. He did not like it very much and he hesitated, about to say something which his personal courage would not let him say. My father, who had been a reading man in the few books he had, often quoted the Bible or other such books, and he was one to speculate on men and their ways. I thought of him now, and wondered what he would say of our situation. Since my father's death I have had no books and read but poorly. It ain't as if the idea wasn't there.

Karpe took his rifle and went out alone, and the rest of us went to work.

It was hot and the air was close. Jim paused once, leaning on his shovel. "Feels like a storm coming," he said, and I did not think he meant only in the weather.

Taking off my guns, I placed them on a flat rock close at hand while I worked. Folks who've never packed pistols can't imagine how heavy they are. Pretty soon Josh Boone got out of

the hole and traded places with Kinyon. Jim, he put down his
rifle and went to work.

All of a sudden, and why I turned I don't know, I turned
sharp around, and there was Ed Karpe standing on the bank
with his rifle in his hands. He was looking down at Boone and
I'd have sworn he was about to shoot him.

Boone, he was on his feet his own rifle ready, and what
would have happened next was anybody's guess, when suddenly an arrow smacked into a tree within inches of Karpe's
head, and he yelled "Injuns!" and ducked for cover.

He took shelter behind the bank while Jim and Boone made
it to the fort. Me, I squatted down in the hole where I was,
and when the Injuns rushed us I opened up with both Colts.
Karpe had turned to fire on them, and what he or the others
did I didn't know, but I dropped four men and a horse. Then I
caught up my rifle, but they were gone, leaving behind them
several horses and some Injuns. A couple of them started to
crawl away, and we let 'em go.

Boone went out to gather up what guns he could find and to
catch up horses and bring 'em in. Whilst he was collectin'
them, I saw him throw something into the bushes. At the time
I thought nothing of it. My guns reloaded, I watched the boys
come together again. Nobody had more than a scratch. We'd
been ready, as much for each other as for them, but everybody
was ready to shoot when they showed up, and of course, we
had our fort, such as it was.

"Lucky!" Boone said. "Mighty lucky!"

"They'll be back," Kinyon replied grimly. "Our scalps are
worth more now that we've shown ourselves warriors."

Nobody knew better than I what a break we'd had. If the
Indians had come at us easy-like, slipping up and opening fire
from cover, we'd have had small chance. Indians have bad
leaders as well as white men, and this one had been too
confident, too eager.

Young braves, no doubt, reckless and anxious to count coup
on a white man, and wanting loot, too, our guns and horses.
But nobody needed to tell anybody what stopped them.

Josh Boone was staring at me again. "You handle them Colts
like a man who knowed how to use 'em."

"Why d' you figure he carries them? I knew he was handy."
Kinyon was smiling with some secret pleasure.

Karpe had a wry amusement in his eyes. "And to think I
nearly got into a shootin' scrape with you!"

"This does it," Kinyon said. "Now we'll have to go."

Boone started to object, then said nothing. We slept cold
that night, staying away from the fire and close to our horses. If
they stole our horses and those we had of theirs, we'd never
get out of here alive. It was too far to anywhere safe.

We slept two at a time, not taking a chance on having just
one man awake, because we didn't know who the murderer
was.

At daybreak we slipped away from camp. We'd covered our
holes, hiding our tools and what gear we did not want to carry.
We kept one pan for taking samples downstream, and then we
took off.

What the others were thinking I had no idea, but as for me,
I was worried. One of us was a murderer and wanted all our
gold. It wasn't enough that we had to watch out for Injuns, but
one amongst us as well.

We hadn't gone three miles before Kinyon, who was in the
lead, threw up a hand. "Injuns!" he said hoarsely. "Must be
thirty or forty of 'em!"

That about-faced us, you can bet! We turned back up-creek,
riding fast, and then turned off into the woods. We hadn't gone
far before we heard 'em again, only this time it was another
bunch already spread out in the woods. A gun thundered
somewhere ahead of us, and then an arrow whistled by my
head, and as I swung my horse I took a quick shot with the
Sharps and saw an Indian fall.

Then I was riding Hell for leather and trying to load whilst
we ran.

There was a yell behind us and Karpe's horse stumbled,
throwing Ed to the ground. He lit running just as a couple of
Indians closed in on him.

One swung a tomahawk high, and I shot without aiming,
then shoved the Sharps into the boot and went for a six-
shooter. Boone and Kinyon both fired, and Ed came running.
He still had his rifle and saddlebags.

"No use to run!" Jim yelled. "Too many of 'em! We've got to stand!"

There were rocks ahead, not far from our old fort, and we hit them running. My horse ran on, but I was shooting soon as I hit the ground, and Kinyon beside me. Boone and Karpe found good places, and they also opened fire. The attack broke off as quick as it began.

Karpe had a bullet scratch along his skull, and a burn on his shoulder. "You boys saved me!" he seemed amazed. "You surely did!"

Our horses were still with us. Mine had run on and then circled back to be with me, or with the horses he knew, I did not know which. We had our horses, but we had Indians all around us and no help nearer than three or four hundred miles. At least, none that we knew of.

"If they wipe us out," Boone commented, "nobody will ever know what happened to us."

"We wouldn't be the first," Kinyon said, "I found a skull and part of a spine and rib cage back yonder when I was huntin' gold. The bones had a gold pan along with 'em."

We sat there waiting for the next attack and expecting little when I heard that stream. It was close by, and in all the confusion I hadn't thought of it. "Look," I said, "if we can hold on until dark, I think I can get us out of this!"

They looked at me, waiting, but nobody said anything. Right at the moment nobody thought much of his chances.

"If we can stand 'em off until dark, we can slip away upstream into a cave I've found. They'll think we've left the country."

"What about our horses?" Kinyon asked.

"Have to leave 'em," I said, although it went hard to leave my Tennessee horse.

"Maybe there's another entrance?" Jim suggested. "Where there's one cave there's sometimes others."

We sat tight and let the sun do its work. It was almighty hot, but we had to put up with it, for there was no more than an edging of shade near some of the boulders. The Injuns tried a few shots and so did we, more to let 'em know we were still alive and ready than with hope of hitting anything.

Boone was lyin' beside me and he kept turning his head to

stare out over the rocks. "Think we'll make it?" he asked me. All the big-headedness seemed to have gone out of him. "I'd sure like to save my pelt."

They came on then. They came in a wave from three sides, riding low on their horses and again it was my Model 48s that stopped them. Not that I killed anybody, but I rained bullets around them and burned a couple, and they couldn't under-stand that rapid fire. They knew about guns, and had some themselves, but they had never run up against any repeating weapons.

The last Injun was riding away when he turned sharp in the saddle and let go with a shot that winged Josh Boone.

It hit him high but hard, and he went down. Leaving the shooting to Karpe and Kinyon, I went to Boone. His face was all twisted with pain, but when I went to undo the laces on his buckskin shirt he jerked away, his eyes wild and crazy. "No! Let me alone! Don't bother with me!"

"Don't be a fool, Josh. You've been hit hard. You get treated or you'll die sure!"

He was sullen. "I'd better die, then. You go off. I'll fix it myself."

Something in his voice stopped me as I started to turn away. Slamming him back on the ground in no gentle way, I ripped open the rawhide cords and peeled back his hunting shirt.

There was a nasty wound there, all right, that had shattered his collar bone and left him bleedin' most awful bad. But that wasn't all.

There was another wound through the top of his shoulder, which was all festerin' and sore. When I saw that I stopped. He stared at me, his mouth drawn in a hard line, his eyes ugly, yet there was something else, too. There was shame as well as fear.

There was only one time he could have gotten that wound. Like when a bullet comes along a man's rifle and cuts the meat atop his shoulder. It had been Josh Boone and not Ed Karpe who had tried to kill Jim Kinyon, and therefore it had been Boone who killed old German Kreuger.

He stared at me and said no word while I washed out the wound, picked away bone fragments, and put it in the best shape I could manage. I folded an old bandana to stop the bleeding, and bound it tight in place. By the time I finished it was fetchin' close to dusk, and the Injuns had let up on their shootin'.

Kinyon guessed right. There was another hole into that cave, just a big crack, like, but big enough to get a horse inside, even a horse as big as my Tennessee. Once they were inside we pulled a couple of pieces of old log into the gap and then we bedded down to wait it out.

Oh, they come a-huntin', all right! We could hear them looking for us, but we kept quiet and after a while they gave up and rode away. We sat it out for three days in that cave, and then Jim slipped out to scout around.

They were gone, thinking we'd gotten away, and we slipped out, mounted up, and headed back for the settlements. When we had buildings in sight and knew we were safe, I pulled up and turned to face them.

"Josh," I said, "German left a widder behind. She's up at this settlement waitin' for him. With German dead, she will be hard put to live. I figure you might like to contribute, Josh."

He sat his horse lookin' at me, and I knew he was left handed as well as right. He had a gun, a handgun I'd seen him pick out of the bushes after he'd taken it off a dead Injun. He looked at me and I looked at him. I put no hand to a gun and I knew there was no need. "You just toss me your poke, Josh," I told him.

His eyes were all mean-like, and he tossed me the poke.

"Now the other one."

Ed Karpe and Jim, they just sat watching and Ed couldn't seem to figure it out. Kinyon knew, although how long he had known I couldn't guess.

Josh Boone waited, holding off as long as he could, but then he tossed me the other poke.

Pocketing the pokes, I then took a couple of nuggets and some dust from my own poke. "There's maybe a hundred dollars there," I said. "It's riding money, a loan from me to you."

"I'll owe you for that," he said. "I always pay my debts."

"I'll see no man beggared with a broken arm," I said, "but that's what I named it. Ridin' money. Now you ride."

We sat there watching while he rode away, back square to us, one arm hitched kind of high. He rode like that right out of time, because we never saw him again.

"Well," Jim said after a bit. "If we ain't campin' here let's ride in. I'm goin' to wet my whistle."

We started riding, and nobody said anything more.